Vi...

"I mean what
the offer if yo...
anythi...
re...

"That's blackmail."

"I know." Mac shouldered his bag and walked a few yards forward to retrieve his golf ball, then walked toward the eighteenth green, leaving her standing still staring after him in stunned anger.

So he thought he could manipulate her, did he? Well, he had a lot to learn about her, then. *I have a lot to learn about myself*, Retta added, *because I can't believe I'm going to do what I'm about to do.*

Retta stalked after him, reckless and single-minded. "McHale, you coward." He turned around, astonished. "You make such a grand show of being alive, but you're not."

He smiled grimly. "Retta, I can be real stubborn . . ." His voice trailed away as she stepped up to him and slid her arms around his neck. Retta looked up at the clubhouse deck. Curious club members looked back.

"I'm going to blow your cover," she said tautly, and kissed him . . .

Jackie Leigh

Jackie Leigh began writing as a youngster in rural Georgia, where her family heritage included Confederate veterans, Cherokee Indians, and gold miners—a history that stirred her imagination.

Journalism seemed the most practical way to channel her energies, and it led to an editing career in medical publications. But she couldn't forget her interest in fiction and decided to try her hand at romances because she had always enjoyed reading them.

Her husband, Hank, an engineer, keeps three cats under control while Jackie writes. In return she helps with carpentry projects for their home in the Georgia mountains. Cooking is their mutual hobby, with dieting a close second.

Dear Reader:

Our August authors draw from their own professional experiences—Christa Merlin as a journalist and Jackie Leigh as a medical editor—to provide vivid, authentic, and sometimes humorous backdrops for their compelling love stories. Both Christa and Jackie have created memorably masterful heroes—a publishing magnate with the kind of potent virility women can't say no to, and a surgeon whose charm and sex appeal rival Dr. Kildare's!

Christa Merlin's hallmarks—convincing characterization and dramatic plots—are impressively displayed in *Accent on Desire* (#420), her fifth Second Chance at Love novel. Investigative reporter Maggie Burton unexpectedly finds herself having close encounters of the deliciously romantic kind with her magnetic new boss, Todd Andrews. Their intimate weekends on Todd's opulent Florida ranch almost lull fiery Maggie into contented domesticity—until she uncovers a scandal literally in Todd's backyard, and issues of trust arise for both of them ... In the tradition of *The Front Page*, Christa colorfully portrays the exciting world of newspaper publishing. Maggie and Todd spar in Hepburn-and-Tracy fashion, and petite readers will especially relish five-foot Maggie's comebacks to quips about her size.

In *Young at Heart* (#421), her fifth Second Chance at Love romance in less than a year (!), amazing Jackie Leigh has written her first book set north of the Mason-Dixon Line. Chicago is where twenty-six-year-old Retta Stanton is swept off her feet by forty-two-year-old cardiologist "Mac" McHale. Jackie displays her renowned humor in the satirical gusto she brings to her depiction of Retta's workplace, and shows emotional power in her portrait of widower Mac coming to terms with his love for a considerably younger woman. Widows and other bereaved readers will identify with Mac's movingly portrayed feelings, and champions of May-December matches will cheer Retta on as she persuades Mac he is indeed young at heart. *Young at Heart* should also have special appeal for medical-romance mavens like ourselves, who still sigh when recalling Rex Morgan, M.D., Ben Casey, or Omar Sharif as Dr. Zhivago.

By the way, both our August authors have won kudos in the romance press. Christa's previous Second Chance at Love novel, *Snowflame*, was awarded four-and-a-half stars by *Affaire de Coeur* (Vol. 6, issue 4), with Mary Nelson's review concluding, "You will find sensuality, sweetness and sadness, so you won't be able to put it down," and Melinda Helfer has pronounced Christa "an extremely satisfying author" (*Romantic Times #27*). Jackie's been a Gold-5 winner from *Barbara's Critiques #81*), and Melinda has lauded her "truly original voice," predicting she'll be "one of the top writers of the genre" (*Romantic Times #36*). And speaking of top romance writers, here's an opportunity to receive, free of charge, an absolute treasure for your romance library—a copy of the bestselling historical novel *The Gamble,* personally inscribed and autographed by much-beloved author LaVyrle Spencer. Just send your name and address on a postcard, indicating you've read this Second Chance at Love "Dear Reader" letter, to Joan Marlow, at the address given at the end of this letter. We'll pick one postcard at random from the first hundred postcards we receive, and we'll mail the writer of that postcard a free, personally incribed copy of *The Gamble.*

It's no gamble but a sure bet that Berkley, the premier romance publisher, offers every romance fan reading pleasure to her personal taste. Our August lineup includes *Prairie*, bestselling-author Anna Lee Waldo's unforgettable saga of the Wild West; *Flame From the Sea*, a steamy tale of fiery Viking passions in mystical medieval Ireland and Norway by Kathryn Kramer; *The Emerald Peacock*, a poignant tale of star-crossed love amid the foothills of the Himalayas in colonial India that's the first novel in Katharine Gordon's Peacock Quartet; the inimitable Barbara Cartland's newest Camfield novel, *Wanted: A Wedding Ring,* set in turn-of-the-century Monte Carlo; and, for Regency fans, ever-popular Elizabeth Mansfield's classic, *Love Lessons.* Also in August, we're proud to be publishing Shirley Lord's *Cosmopolitan* Novel-of-the-Month, *One of My Very Best Friends*, a chronicle of two girl friends who grow up together on the drab streets of London's East End in the 1950's, and become arch rivals amid the luxurious mansions of the Bahamas, Palm Beach, New York, and California in the 1970's.

Happy reading!

With best wishes—

Joan Marlow

Joan Marlow, Editor
Second Chance at Love
The Berkley Publishing Group
200 Madison Avenue
New York, NY 10016

SECOND CHANCE AT LOVE™

JACKIE LEIGH
YOUNG AT HEART

BERKLEY BOOKS, NEW YORK

For Ann and George, who
proved that golf can be
very romantic.

First edition published August 1987

ISBN: 0-425-10516-4

"Second Chance at Love" and the butterfly emblem are trademarks belonging to Jove Publications, Inc. The name "BERKLEY" and the "B"
logo are trademarks belonging to Berkley Publishing Corporation.

Second Chance at Love books are published by
The Berkley Publishing Group
200 Madison Avenue, New York, NY 10016

Printed in the United States of America

10 9 8 7 6 5 4 3 2 1

CHAPTER ONE

DR. KILDARE, EAT your heart out.

Retta Stanton issued that silent challenge to the fictional TV physician as she listened to an incomparable male voice, a wonderful baritone. It belonged to the real-life physician who stood somewhere on the dark stage nearly a hundred feet in front of her. Dr. Bronson McHale's voice resonated through the conference hall of the Chicago Marriot with a sensual richness that was both soothing and erotic.

Her eyes closed, Retta imagined that voice speaking her name. Inside her sensible support panty hose, her knees quivered. Marcus Welby's dulcet tones paled in comparison. Ben Casey and his dreamy voice could take a hike. She kept her eyes closed and for a few moments let her lonely, serious world disappear in a sensual fantasy.

A few seats down from her a physician rattled a cup full of ice and guffawed at something Dr. McHale said. Retta realized that she hadn't heard a word of the joke because she wasn't listening to his speech, only to his voice. Her fantasy evaporated and she opened her eyes quickly, all business once again.

"I'm getting lonely and eccentric in my old age," Retta muttered under her breath. "And I'm only twenty-six. It's just a man making a speech. Good Lord."

But Dr. McHale's voice was the sexiest voice she'd ever

heard in her life. It soared with enthusiasm and humor. It coated highly clinical terms such as "laser ablation" and "cardiac arrhythmias" with an animated midwestern drawl that made them sound comfortably folksy.

Hi there, had a laser ablation lately? a person could casually ask someone after hearing Dr. McHale discuss the procedure. How you doin'? What a nice cardiac arrhythmia.

Retta smiled ruefully at her uncharacteristic whimsy and tilted her head to catch every note of his presentation. Complicated charts and explicit photographs of pig hearts flashed across the two huge screens on the stage. Dr. McHale cracked another joke, and the cavernous meeting hall reverberated with the laughter of approximately five hundred of his fellow physicians.

Retta laughed, too, her soft voice high and almost giddy. She wasn't accustomed to hearing herself make such a strange, unprofessional noise, and it startled her. Abruptly clamping her mouth shut, she glanced around furtively as if people might be staring. They weren't, thank goodness.

I'm simply a slave to those gentle, deep, Jimmy Stewart—endearing inflections of his, she admitted. She felt warm all over, and her cheeks tingled with a flush of attraction. I just know that he's built like a pear and has no chin, Retta added with typical pragmatic reasoning. She'd come into the hall in the dark, after his speech had begun, and she couldn't even see his silhouette to gather a clue to his appearance.

". . . so we have great hope that this technique will be a successful adjunct to, if not a replacement for, balloon angioplasty," the mysterious Dr. McHale finished. "Our pig subjects came through the procedure with flying colors." He paused dramatically. "They didn't survive the celebration barbecue, however. . . ."

Retta smiled again as the audience laughed and applauded, drowning out Dr. McHale's concluding "thank you." Perched on the edge of her folding chair, she leaned into the darkness with an uncustomary show of anxiety, her strong hands knotted into the gray skirt she wore and her eyes locked on the stage.

Now, Retta thought grimly, as the lights began to flicker. Now I'll see what he looks like and get this silly infatuation out of my system. She knew a great deal about him from the articles she'd read, but she'd never seen a photograph. The lights came up. Her heart rate went with them.

Henrietta Pauline Stanton, who rarely allowed herself to be so outwardly exuberant, nearly burst with a slow smile of wonder. The man on the stage bore no resemblance to a pear. He had a definite chin, and . . . he lived up to the mesmerizing promise in his voice. She sighed, hypnotized. On rare occasions, dreams could come true.

Mac McHale scanned the audience and felt pride rise inside his chest as the applause continued longer and louder than the standard polite patter most speakers received. *Yep,* he thought, *I owe myself a cigar for this one. They loved it.*

"Dr. McHale will be available for questions during the next fifteen minutes," announced the conference moderator, a stout, balding physician wearing a brown suit with a red bow tie. "This concludes today's agenda for the American Academy of Cardiologists. Enjoy the Chicago nightlife and try not to get caught in any April showers."

Mac started down the short flight of steps that led to the carpeted floor of the hall, and the other man followed him, slapping his shoulder.

"Great damn job, Mac, old buddy," he proclaimed. "You not only had a top-notch study, you sold it with showmanship. As always."

"Nobody said pig hearts have to be dull, Vince."

"They're not *Playboy* material either, though."

Grinning and relaxed, Mac stepped into the midst of a crowd of physicians who were pushing forward, eager to ask questions. He quickly lost himself in answering them, discussing the study with the same easy-natured but serious attitude he'd employed during the formal presentation. Vince disappeared in search of the first of the several happy-hour bourbons Mac knew he would have.

Fifteen minutes flew by, and Mac had just finished answering the earnest question of a young Indian physician when Vince sauntered up and bumped his elbow with a tumbler full of ice and amber liquid.

"Let's blow this joint, McHale." Mac raised a distracted hand as he finished answering a new question, his eyes trained on the physician who'd asked it. Vince waved his drink at the small group still waiting. "You gentlemen come on down to the hotel bar if you can't stand to part with this big clown. Oh, I should say you gentlemen and lady."

". . . and that's why I feel confident the technique can be used on humans." Mac's eyes flickered up at Vince in curiosity. Lady? There weren't many female cardiologists, and he admired any woman determined enough to combat the field's male hierarchy.

Mac glanced at the half dozen people standing around him and saw nothing but an assortment of men. Then his gaze swung to his right. And froze.

"Dr. McHale, I'd like to introduce myself," she began quietly. She extended a hand without hesitation, her eyes somber, her shoulders squared under a strictly tailored gray suit with a simple white blouse.

"Introductions can take place down in the bar," Vince interrupted. "We need a good-looking woman with us. Come on down there."

"Don't pay any attention to this old cretin," Mac told her, nodding toward Vince. Then he simply stood there, as he felt the megawatt power of her serious hazel gaze sapping his composure, his concentration, and his ability to move.

Retta's hand wavered, and embarrassment tinged her gaze. Why is he staring at me as if I'm a white elephant at the zoo? she wondered nervously. Please don't let him be patronizing or arrogant toward women. She knew her youthful appearance often put her at a disadvantage. Physicians never took her seriously at first.

Her mouth tightened in defense and she started to withdraw her hand. Mac saw the vulnerable look of retreat on her face and hurriedly gathered his wits. She wasn't a doctor, she was too young. Maybe a student, but she couldn't be more than about twenty-five years old.

"I . . . here," he mumbled, and grasped her hand.

Her fingers were warm and her grip held his with strength and assurance. The skin of her palm was dotted with intriguing calluses—probably from long hours holding a tennis racket, he thought. Only she didn't look like the kind who played tennis. She looked as if she never wore anything but wool business suits. God, he'd forgotten how a woman could make a man's mind wander.

But this wasn't just any woman. This was the most eye-catching woman he'd ever met. *But too damned young.* Mac cleared his throat, let go of her hand, and tried to form a relaxed, friendly smile.

"What can I do for you?" he asked.

Just keep smiling at me, Retta thought. For a moment he'd looked shocked—stern—and she'd expected the worst. Although she was five feet seven he towered over her, and the combination of his height and his aura of confidence had been lethally disconcerting.

"I thought your presentation was fascinating," she said. There was no indication of flattery in her voice, just solemn fact. "Are you using lasers for anything other than research?"

"Why don't the pretty ones ever ask *me* questions?" Vince wanted to know. Mac cocked one sandy brown eyebrow at him in rebuke, then looked back at her.

"I'm afraid the uses for cardiology are still experimental," he explained. "But I do a great job of slicing the skin off a grapefruit with a C-O Two laser. I'm real proud of that."

The men standing around them chuckled. She nodded politely. The humor gleaming in her eyes was the only indication that she appreciated his attempt at a joke. Mac pushed his sports jacket open and shoved his hands in his slacks pockets to quell the urge he had to fidget like an overeager kid talking to his first girl friend. Someone asked him a question and he glanced away, answering it.

He's very down to earth, she thought with relief. Her heart quit leaping about her rib cage like a deranged rabbit and settled into a more normal rhythm as she used the free moment to study him intently.

He had rich brown hair cut short to keep its thick layers in a neat style. On the sides it lightened from gold to distinctive gray as it spread back from his temples. Except for the evidence of age in his hair and the maturity that framed his straight, lean features with faint lines, he could have passed for a doctor not long out of medical school instead of a prominent cardiologist with a long history of achievement.

Suddenly he turned his gaze back to her—directly, disarmingly back—as if his attention had never really left her during his conversation with the other person. Retta's stomach tingled and dropped in response.

Dr. Kildare had never had this effect. Of course, she'd been in grammar school then.

"I got sidetracked," he said. "I apologize. Tell me your name."

"I'm Retta Stanton. I called your receptionist earlier this week and she told me I could find you at the conference today. I'm with National Health Publishing. She said she'd give you my message."

"National Health, yes. I remember." He barely remembered because it'd been a busy week, but he wasn't going to hurt her feelings by saying so. "The company's based here in Chicago, isn't it?"

"Yes, our offices are just off Michigan Avenue. We publish monthly newsletters for physicians, and we're planning a new one called *Ethics in Health Care*."

"National Health is Newt Winston's outfit," Vince interjected with a blustery laugh. "You've heard of him, haven't you, Mac? The dermatologist who made a mint by inventing ChapAway? A research guy. Never practiced medicine a day in his life. Now he's a publisher."

"I'm afraid I don't know him," Mac admitted. He noticed a trace of rueful discomfort in Retta Stanton's face, as if she were woefully accustomed to hearing physicians bandy her employer's name the way Vince had.

"But I use ChapAway all the time," Mac lied. He felt inordinately pleased when his remark drove the discomfort out of her expression.

"On your pigs?" she quipped.

Mac chuckled, liking her composure, his instinct telling him that she might be someone he could like very much on short notice.

"They're not my pigs," he answered with mock sternness. "They belong to the Center for Laser Research over in Springfield. But I bet ChapAway would work very well on pigs. Their skin's very similar to human skin, as I'm sure you know."

"You're saying that you really can make a silk purse out of a sow's ear?"

"I haven't done the silk purse study yet."

He laughed deeply at their repartee, but she allowed only a pleased, proper smile. It hinted at more boisterous humor under the surface, but how far under he couldn't be sure. She was very solemn, especially for such a young person.

"Mac, let's go," Vince interrupted. "Pigs, schmigs, the hotel has a ten-cent oyster bar downstairs."

The physicians still waiting to ask questions shuffled impatiently and looked at their watches. Mac saw Retta Stanton glance at them defensively. A slight furrow appeared between her luxurious brown eyebrows, which were several shades darker than her cocoa-colored hair.

That hair fascinated him. It was thick and lustrous, but she wore it regimented in precisely arranged layers swept away from her face and curved in a rigid formation just touching the back of her blouse collar. Snap to, soldier! that hair told the world.

"Just hold on, Vince," he ordered. "Let your blood pressure simmer."

She gave him a grateful look and he nodded, distracted. She had an intelligent, square-jawed face, and her brows lent it a dramatic dimension. Mac decided that she wasn't conventionally beautiful, but she was infinitely fascinating. He suspected he'd see her face in his dreams. The rest of her, slender and well proportioned under that rigid, unappealing business suit, would float through his lonely dreams as well.

"Why don't you come downstairs with us," he offered in a neutral voice. "And whatever it is that you want to discuss, we can discuss after I answer a few questions for these gentlemen."

"I have to get back to the office," she answered. He heard a twinge of sincere regret in her tone. "Can I reach you by phone next week?"

"Mac's no fun," Vince told her coyly. "Don't call him. Call me in my hotel room tonight. I'll talk to you about anything, baby."

Mac felt an uncharacteristic surge of protective anger, as if Vince had just insulted someone very important to him. Vince loved young women, and he had three ex-wives who'd confirm it. Mac shot him a glare and started to remind him that they were attending a conference, not a singles' weekend for older men.

"Pardon me, have we been introduced?" Retta Stanton asked Vince politely. Mac watched her slender fingers, which ended in neat, blunt nails slicked with clear polish, curl over the clasp of a gray clutch purse. That's a predatory gesture, he thought with amusement. Watch out, Vince.

"Vince Satterfield," Vince rejoined, and stuck out a hand made hard from many afternoons of golf. "And if you're not a doctor, you should be. We've got too many feminist broads with big fannies and buck teeth in this profession. You'd be a pretty change."

Retta shook his hand firmly, professionally. She had the panache of a much older person, Mac thought again. She might look young, but she wasn't going to be buffaloed by his rowdy companion. Her composure continued to impress him.

"Dr. Satterfield," she said softly. "Let's get something straight. I'm assistant executive editor of a national publishing company. I'm not here to endure your snide remarks about women. And although I'm an editor, not a physician, I find your attitude toward female physicians offensive."

In an attempt to hide his smile, Mac pressed his lips together so tightly that he was afraid they must be turning white. He watched the coyness drain out of Vince's face. Satterfield's expression confirmed that he'd just had the wind removed from his sexist sails.

"I apologize," Vince said stiffly. Several doctors in the group studiously trained their attention on interesting parts of the chandeliered ceiling, humor barely concealed on their faces. "Excuse me." He tucked his chin and growled at the assembled group. "Let's us male chauvinists take ourselves downstairs before somebody does laser surgery on our pig hearts. We'll see you there, McHale."

The group followed him as he stomped off toward one in a series of double doors on the side of the conference hall. For an awkward, silent moment, Retta looked after them.

"I can be very blunt," she said. "I hope you understand why I had to say what I said."

"I do entirely. I was . . . embarrassed . . . by my friend's attitude." She looked at him in pleased surprise, which provoked a new feeling of protectiveness in him. Mac told himself firmly that his emotion was paternal. "Come on, walk with me downstairs and let's talk on the way," he said abruptly, gesturing toward the doors with one hand. "And don't pay any attention to Vince. He's forty-five going on twelve. Harmless, but annoying sometimes."

"I'm sorry, but I don't have a sense of humor about these things. I have to insist on professional treatment if I'm going to do a good job."

She wasn't offended, just frank. Mac couldn't resist testing the formal facade she presented.

"You should have a sense of humor about things that don't matter. What makes you laugh?"

He altered his lanky strides to match her shorter ones as they left the hall and entered a communal area filled with cardiology exhibits from medical supply firms. Retta fumbled with her purse, moving it from under one arm to the other.

"I . . . ummm . . ." Dammit, she couldn't think of one thing. Am I that dull? she wondered suddenly. "You," she said finally.

"Me?" He looked down at her as they walked through the crowded exhibit area. She kept her gaze straight ahead and nodded, her firm, determined chin thrust forward as if she were obstinate about the fact that she found him funny.

"Your presentation. You have a way of lightening a serious subject without sounding flippant. You'd make a great teacher."

"Why, thank you." Mac took compliments with a grain of salt, ordinarily. He was so at ease with himself that he didn't let other people's opinions affect him much either way. But now he felt a rush of pleasure at her simple comment. "Say, you wouldn't just be angling for a free drink, would you?"

"Oh, no. I . . . no." She was so perturbed that he knew she'd failed to hear the teasing note in his voice. Well, he had been serious about the drink, but he hadn't known a better way to ask her to have a drink with him, so he'd floundered around with a joke that hadn't worked and now he felt ridiculous—something he rarely felt. Mac frowned.

"What do you need to talk to me about, Ms. Stanton?"

"Well, Dr. Winston, my . . ."—she smiled ruefully— "infamous boss feels that you're one of the country's leading experts on ethics issues. He knows that you're codirector of the ethics committee at Rush-Presbyterian and he saw the *Today* show interview in which you discussed living wills. I'd like to discuss our new ethics newsletter with you; Dr. Winston would like for you to head the advisory board."

"Whoa," Mac said immediately. They had entered an atrium area centered around flights of escalators. Not sure whether it was a rhetorical "whoa" or not, she stopped. He stopped also, looking down at her with intense, curious eyes.

Gray-blue eyes, she noticed suddenly. Warm, inviting eyes, youthful in a weathered face that had obviously spent many hours in the sun and wind. Athletic hours, if the trim body outlined by the handsome houndstooth jacket and gray slacks was any indication.

"I'm honored," he said sincerely. "But it sounds pretty involved. I can't give you an answer here at the head of the escalators—or even at the foot of the escalators. We need to discuss this in detail."

"Believe me, I understand. Dr. Winston would like to get together with you for lunch next week."

To hell with Newt Winston, Marc thought abruptly. I want to have lunch with you. He kicked himself mentally for admitting that. He had no intention of traipsing after a woman nearly young enough to be his daughter. That was the kind of embarrassing thing Vince did.

Retta stared up at him, caught in his mesmerizing gaze, not knowing how to judge its mixture of scrutiny and regret.

"Can't you come downstairs to the hotel bar for just a few minutes?" Mac asked. He couldn't help himself. Was it selfish to want to bask in the company of a fascinating woman, no matter what her age? "I'm not trying to be coy, I really would like to discuss this business with you."

"I'd love to, but I really do have to get back to the office to take care of some paperwork."

"It's after five. What kind of sweatshop does Mr. Chap-Away run?"

A smile that bordered on weariness edged her mouth. "A white-collar sweatshop."

They began to walk again by silent, mutual agreement. She stepped onto an escalator and he followed. Retta stood on the step just beneath his and very carefully kept her gaze forward. He made an overwhelming impression on her hormones as it was, and she feared that if she kept staring at him unabashedly, those hormones might never return to normal levels.

Retta decided that, were she a frivolous person, she'd be tempted to give a moment's consideration to the sickly sweet term, "love at first sight," but, being the realistic and highly logical person she was, she wondered instead if he wore one of those new colognes that provoked female chemicals to react. She sniffed subtly. No clue.

"Well, we have to figure out when we can meet to talk," Mac said. Hmmm . . . let me think."

In the process he reached inside his jacket and retrieved a dark blue handkerchief, which he flourished with a little snap of his wrist. Retta turned surprised eyes on him as he rolled the handkerchief into a wad and tucked it into his closed fist. "Say the magic words," he commanded.

Her eyes widened.

"What are they?"

Mac gave her a look of mock dismay. "You don't know any magic words? How do you get through the day?"

She shook her head as if she wasn't certain how, and he saw something wistful and chagrined pass across her expression. It touched him deeply. He wondered if she was happy under that solemn, controlled exterior.

"Well, 'abracadabra' will do."

"Abracadabra," she offered lamely.

He opened his hand to reveal one of his business cards where the handkerchief had resided a moment earlier. A slow smile spread across her face, warming it, making Mac's breath stop in his throat. She looked up at him with sheer admiration in her eyes.

"That was marvelous, Dr. McHale."

They reached the bottom of the escalator and stepped off. Disconcerted, he handed her the card and bowed.

"What other tricks do you do?" Retta blurted, then felt heat zinging up to her cheeks. *I can't believe I said that*, she moaned inwardly.

His head jerked up. He looked amused, but just as startled as she knew she did.

"I mean," she tried desperately, "is that the only trick you do in public . . ." Her voice trailed off. Mortified, she clamped her mouth shut.

"I, uh, eat dinner well." Mac saw her discomfort, and realized that she wasn't nearly as unflappable as she'd like

everyone to believe. Dammit, he wanted to know more
about her. He spoke carefully. "Would you like to . . . no, I
know it's short notice. I just thought we could talk about
the . . . what was that newsletter again?"

"Ethics," she mumbled, and looked away. Ask, ask, she
urged him silently. Ask me to dinner.

"Well, call me, and we'll set up a lunch meeting with
the infamous Dr. Winston. I might be interested in the
project."

"Good."

They shared another long look. Mac finally broke the
enchantment and held out his hand. She shook it with a
quick, professional squeeze and let go.

"It was nice meeting you," he said sincerely. She nodded.

"Thank you for your interest. In the newsletter, I
mean." Retta took a step backward, wincing at the strange
way her tongue seemed to be producing innuendos without
her permission. "I'll call you, Dr. McHale."

"It's Mac. Please."

"Call me Retta . . . please."

She gave him one last nod, turned on her heels, and
walked toward the street exit, her back very straight. Mac
watched her until she disappeared through the swinging
glass doors.

His head down and his hands sunk into his pockets, he
turned to walk toward the bar. Loneliness gripped him in a
way it hadn't in ages. Judith had been dead four years, and
in that time he couldn't remember having felt this isolated
before.

He had almost reached the bar's entrance when he became aware of heels clicking to a stop on the marble floor
behind him. Mac turned around glumly. Retta Stanton
looked up at him with calm serious eyes.

"Mac," she said evenly. "Could you go to dinner tonight? My company will pay. You and I could meet somewhere and talk about the newsletter."

The pleasure that eased into his face squelched every
horrible fear she'd had that he'd fumble for a polite way to

refuse. Now her nerves could quit snapping like violin strings. It had taken all her considerable courage to walk back in and ask him to dinner.

"Good enough. How about seven o'clock?"

"Fine." She felt weak with anticipation. "Do you like Barney's Market Club, over on Randolph Street?"

"That's a fairly expensive dinner for a business meeting. Are you sure, Ms. . . . Retta?"

"Dr. Winston would want you to have a nice dinner," she said solemnly.

"He's a grand guy, I can just tell." Mac knew he must be grinning like an idiot, but he'd never been much good at hiding happiness. At hiding unhappiness, he was a pro. "Then I'll see you at seven, at Barney's."

"Great." She hesitated, looking up at him, looking pleased because he'd accepted her invitation. The she held out her hand again. He shook it again.

Neither of them let go.

"Mac, get yourself on in here . . . whoops." Vince stopped outside the bar, a fresh drink in his hand. Retta and Mac stepped back and quit shaking—no, holding—hands. She fumbled with her purse, opening it and rummaging busily for something. Mac straightened his dark blue tie, which didn't need straightening.

"Well," Vince huffed, "am I still in disfavor, young lady?"

Retta looked up at him. "That's young woman," she answered. But a corner of her mouth crooked up. Who had time to hold grudges against sexist doctors? Retta was suddenly feeling very magnanimous—and oddly like laughing. "No."

"Thank God!" They exchanged droll looks for a moment.

She finished going through her purse and handed first Vince and then Mac her boldly colored business card. Mac looked at it quizzically, and his mouth twitched with humor.

"I look forward to dinner, Henrietta P. Stanton." Her mouth thinned at his gently teasing tone.

"I do too, Bronson Amadeus."

She nodded at his shocked expression, smiled slightly, then swung around and headed back toward the exit, her stride sturdy and graceful, her head up. Mac stared after her blankly. Beside him, Vince began to laugh.

"How do you think she found out about my middle name?" Mac asked. "She must have really checked me out before she came here today."

Vince clapped a hand to his forehead, rocked back and forth on his crepe soles, and laughed harder. When he spoke, his words were breathless with chortles.

"McHale, you've been ignoring women ever since your wife died. I think you've just met your match."

Mac's face turned grim.

"No," he said tautly, still looking toward the door where he'd last seen Retta Stanton. "Not with that young woman. You're wrong."

CHAPTER TWO

THE AFTER-FIVE CROWD at National Health Publishing was as frayed and crazy as ever when Retta pushed open the door to the upstairs suite that contained the bustling editorial department.

"Go out for a pass!" an airy female voice cried from somewhere down the hall that circled the perimeter of the tiny offices. Retta recognized it as belonging to Vanessa Riley, a petite and deceptively delicate-looking managing editor.

"Yoooow-weeee!" an excited male voice responded. Retta heard running footsteps. Bob Mauldin—a stocky, bearded blond with a lovable Santa Claus personality—burst into the department reception area just as a foam rubber football sailed into view over his head. With a mighty leap he caught the missile and staggered to a stop by a potted corn plant. He grinned at Retta.

"The demi-boss is here!" he yelled in Vanessa's direction, but hurled the football at Retta. She caught it with one hand and sent it back with a graceful underhand toss.

"I suppose this game means your interview still hasn't called you back, Bob." She gazed at him sternly but without malice, as if he were a lovable though misbehaving puppy. Retta's instinctive management sense had long ago taught her the value of letting the editors enjoy their rowdy diversions. Playing kept them sane, helped them bear the fierce workload. They repayed her with a teasing devotion that she secretly enjoyed. Bob sighed dramatically.

"You're right, my dear. I guess it's going to be another lovely Wednesday night waiting by the phone. It ain't easy being the country's 'information chef' on AIDS."

"Who called you that?" she asked, although she could easily guess.

"Newt."

Their publisher talked in food analogies. Some businessmen used sports metaphors; Newt used food. He was eccentric and maddening and brilliant, which made him successful but only occasionally likable. He turned a suspicious eye on any employee who left on time at the end of the day, and frequently stopped by on weekends just to see who was dedicated and who wasn't.

"Hi Leila," Retta said as she passed an open door. Inside, a slender young woman with bristly punk-orange hair looked up from her computer terminal and saluted. "How's it going?"

"I'm zoned to the max," Leila muttered, and slid a headset over the numerous pieces of jewelry in each of her ears. "Transcribing tapes is a drag. I feel like a waste-oid."

"A what?"

"A zoned-out dweeb."

"Ah. I understand," Retta lied.

"No you don't, sweetcakes. But you care, and that's the important thing. Nobody else gives a flying dip."

"Let me know if I can do something to help, Leila."

"My gray matter is beyond help. Beyond. Besides, you're already maxed out with the drabs and the duties."

Retta nodded in acknowledgement of that fact, and continued down the hall. On days like this she wondered why she cared so much about her job, and why she'd been at National Health Publishing for nearly four years, when few editors made it past two.

The money was decent, of course, and that was a prime reason. After growing up poor, she relished her modest security. But on nights when depression caught up with her, she admitted that she also stayed because she had too many empty spaces in her life, and the demands of her job helped her ignore them.

But she didn't dwell on those thoughts today. Today, she had too much crackling energy in her to brood. Retta hurried down a hallway to the relatively comfortable office her position granted her, and settled in the nubby green confines of her desk chair. Immediately her phone buzzed.

"Retta!" Newt boomed over its speaker in his godlike voice. She picked up the receiver for privacy.

"Hello."

"Did he say yes?"

"Not yet. But he's interested."

"We have to have Dr. McHale, Retta. He's the biggest potato in the ethics field. Without him, the newsletter won't have nearly the same spice."

"I'm buying him dinner tonight. We're going to talk."

"Good. Mingle. Pick his brain like a ripe crop. Where are you having dinner?"

"Barney's."

"Good, good. Call me first thing in the morning with a report." Click. Retta looked down at the receiver and grimaced comically.

She'd worked hard to rise to assistant executive editor, the second most important position in the editorial department, and she played by the company rules. But she had the good management sense to maintain a healthy dose of independence that kept the harried editors on her side.

Scott Woodruff, the company computer wizard and a managing editor—there were two, he and Vanessa—stuck his handsome face in at her door. She gazed up in welcome. She and Scott were best friends, a relationship that seemed odd to everyone but the two of them.

He was thirty years old, just marking time at National Health until he finished his masters in health science. Scott had magnificent pecan-colored hair and a gorgeous body —and about a dozen "lady friends." Retta liked being different from that group.

A definite undercurrent of flirtatious male-female feelings ran between them, but neither she nor Scott wanted those to intrude on a dynamic and very comfortable friendship.

"McHale was great, I bet," he prodded. Retta nodded dreamily. A wicked smile slid across Scott's face.

"Oh-ho. Better than great."

"Take your insinuations elsewhere," she ordered without true malice. "Thanks for checking all those cardiology indexes for articles he's written. I learned a lot about him from them, and I think it made me feel more comfortable today."

"I found a new article this afternoon. Personal stuff. He got into the ethics field after his wife died of leukemia. Four years ago. She was on total life support for the last six weeks, and he hated it. That's why he's a big proponent of 'do not resuscitate' sanctions." Scott glanced at his watch. "Geez, gotta go. I've got a bike club meeting tonight."

"Wait!" She half rose from her chair. "What else did you find out about him?"

"That's about it. I put the article in your mailbox."

"Thanks. Thanks a lot, Scott."

Retta waited impatiently until she heard the back door that led to the fire escape—everyone's regular route of exit—slam, signaling Scott's departure. Then she virtually ran down the hall to the communal area where the copier and mail boxes sat on a long table against one wall.

"Wife's Death Prompts Cardiologist To Question Health Care Ethics," the article was titled. Retta clasped it tightly and began devouring the words as she walked back to her office. Seated at her desk a few minutes later she laid the shiny Xerox copy down and swiveled her chair so she could look at the Chicago street outside. She hardly saw it.

"Poor McHale," she whispered gently.

The ornate oak bar at Barney's Market Club was, like the restaurant itself, a Chicago institution. Dark and comfortable, the 1919 tin ceiling still in place, the restaurant was the quintessential old Chicago steak house.

Retta saw Mac leaning against the bar with his back to her, and she took a moment to gather her reserve and her breath. From her research she knew his age, forty-two. That made him sixteen years her senior, but it didn't matter. This man was special, and besides, everything about him bespoke a perpetual youth——his laughter, his lack of pretense, the healthy virility he radiated.

The bartender and Mac were laughing. She watched in amazement as Mac tucked a pack of cards back in some inner pocket of his sports coat. A cardiologist who performed sleight of hand——she hadn't yet analyzed the full irony of his nature. Mac turned around at almost the same second that she reached his elbow, and her carefully modulated calm deserted her.

"Hi!" she chirped. He looked down at her with a subdued, oddly troubled expression on his face for a moment. Then a polite smile curved his mouth.

"Hello, Henrietta."

"Amadeus."

They traded benignly challenging looks as the bartender asked what Retta wanted to drink. She looked at the glass in Mac's hand. He followed her gaze.

"Milk," he said, without embarrassment. Retta nodded, pursing her lips as she assessed this interesting tidbit about his preferences. An unusual man, this fellow.

"I'll have milk, too," she told the bartender. He gave them both a raised eyebrow but said nothing. Retta looked up and caught Mac studying her, his head tilted to one side. She swallowed hard and tried to ignore the hard thumping of her heart without success.

"All right, Henrietta, how do you know my middle name?" Mac asked abruptly.

"I did some background research on you in connection with the newsletter. An old article in *Cardiology Alert* mentioned your full name."

"That article was written years ago!"

"Dr. Winston insists on a thorough background check of all potential advisory board members."

"Why? Is he paranoid?"

"Yes."

Mac studied the solemn expression on her face, thinking

that she was kidding, then realizing that she wasn't. She appeared to be serious about almost everything.

"Do you mind if I ask why your parents named you Amadeus?" she asked. The bartender handed her a glass of milk and she took one slow sip, then set the glass and her purse down and clasped her hands in front of her with all the primness of someone's elderly maiden aunt. Mac didn't want to feel drawn to her, but he found her somber, little-old-lady mannerisms endearing.

"My folks either wanted me to be a composer or an Austrian," he quipped. "I was never sure which."

She had a full, enticing mouth that couldn't look stern for long no matter how hard she tried. Now its corners moved with involuntary humor.

"Do you dislike the name?"

"It wasn't any fun growing up in an Idaho farm community with a name like Amadeus. Or Bronson. So I became Mac at an early age." He paused. "Where did you grow up, Henrietta?"

"South of here, in Springfield." She studiously ignored his insistent use of her full name, which had never sounded so silly as when he spoke it in his mock-serious voice.

"Ah, a native of Illinois. A farm girl?"

"No. I moved to Chicago when I was ten, to live with my Aunt Desinada."

"Our families shared the same penchant for odd names," he teased.

"Desinada deserved an odd name. She had an odd way of looking at things. She used to tell people that I was her midget sister. We had a lot of fun with that game."

"Your parents . . ." he probed, and let his voice trail off.

"They died in a boating accident." She said the words with an unruffled frankness that made them sound nonchalant. It had been a long time, after all, and the searing old pain only surfaced occasionally during bad dreams.

But the gentle, sympathetic look that crept over his handsome face made goose bumps rise on her arms. Without a word he conveyed understanding and sorrow. Retta quickly took another sip of her milk.

"So you lived here in Chicago with your Aunt Desinada," he said softly. Retta nodded.

"She was a secretary for the phone company. We had an apartment here in town, the Near North section."

"Was? Had?"

"She died a couple of years ago. Kidney disease. I moved to a smaller place."

His eyes narrowed. No wonder she had such an old attitude about her. She'd experienced more grief than the average person her age. She glanced up at him, then looked away. She wore virtually no makeup, but her dramatic coloring obscured the need. Her dark brown lashes quivered as she looked down at her milk. Mac's hand gripped the warm, old wood of the bar. Without much provocation he could have taken her in his arms and hugged her.

What a ridiculous urge to feel toward a woman he barely knew. He believed in hugging and hugged often among both male and female friends, and with his college-age son, Lucas. Hugging had therapeutic qualities.

Mac wondered drolly what Retta Stanton would do if he used that reasoning and hugged her. He was certain he'd need therapy afterward for the verbal scalding she'd give him, just like the one she'd given Vince.

Retta studied his frown and decided he was sorry he'd inquired into her background.

"Good heavens, I don't mean to sound so melodramatic," she hurried to say. "I was very lucky to have three terrific people to love. Let's change the subject."

"It's all right. You sound brave, not melodramatic." She didn't want sympathy, but he had a feeling that she needed sympathy. Mac was struck again with the sense of protectiveness he'd had when Vince flirted with her. "Do you have any other family?"

"Oh, a few cousins, aunts, and uncles. They're scattered. None of them live in Illinois."

It occurred to him that she might be married. He checked her left hand as casually as he could. No ring, but that didn't mean anything. Why should it matter to me? he demanded silently. She's too young. He had to keep reminding himself of that. This is purely a business meeting, McHale.

Mac reacted the way he always reacted when he was disturbed and confused. He bluffed. Retta blinked in surprise and drew a sharp breath as his hand suddenly darted forward.

For a split second his fingertips brushed the tender skin behind her right ear. The coarse material of his jacket sleeve brushed her cheek, and she caught a whiff of crisp, energizing cologne. When he pulled his hand back he held a neatly folded five-dollar bill between his thumb and forefinger.

"Thank you," he said cheerfully, "for buying the milk." He dropped the bill on the bar and nodded toward the exit. "Let's go get a table."

Retta looked at him open-mouthed. Then a soft explosion of mirth burst from her lips.

"You can't pay. Dr. Winston is paying."

"Dr. Winston is bribing. I have to retain a shred of honor." He faked a look of chagrin. "What kind of guy do you think I am?"

She smiled at him. My kind, she thought, as she walked out of the bar with him close by her side.

Dinner at Barney's could never be a light, low-calorie affair. The menu consisted primarily of barbecued ribs, prime rib, steaks, and lobster. Seated at a quiet table, they avoided anything but chitchat until after they ordered their meals. She asked for a Tom Collins, and he requested a beer. After the waiter left Retta steepled her hands in front of her on the table and pinned him with a no-nonsense gaze.

"Let me give you a little history on National Health . . ." she started.

"Old Newt peddles thirty different newsletters and a dozen conferences to physicians and other medical people all over the country," Mac continued grandly. "He has about a hundred employees and almost as many lady friends. He's fifty-six years old and never married, and he collects porcelain clown figurines." Mac leaned back with an expression of enormous self-satisfaction.

Retta looked at him with exaggerated suspicion.

"You did some investigating of your own, I see. Turnabout is fair play?"

He nodded and laughed. His laugh was hearty, deep, and full. It squinted his denim-colored eyes and made them gleam. It was irresistible.

When Mac stopped laughing he found her eyes trained on him. She had leaned forward slightly and cocked her head on one side. The dim restaurant lights picked up copper highlights in her shiny, chocolate hair, and her eyes were as dark as mahogany.

Some emotion had softened her strong face into a wistful, beautiful expression. His laughter drained away as he nearly melted inside.

"I learned some things about you, too, Henrietta," he told her. His voice came out gruff and low, which he hadn't expected. Mac cleared his throat.

She straightened and eyed him with the wary look of a very private person.

"Who's your source?"

"Larry Burdine."

"Ah." Burdine, who now headed public relations for the American Academy of Cardiologists, had started at National Health the same month as herself. They'd been editors together.

"I saw Burdine in the Marriott bar after you left. I figured all you writing people know each other somehow or other. Surprise. He worked for Newt a year."

"And what awful lies did he tell you about me?" she joked.

Mac rubbed his hands together in a quick movement. From somewhere came a dewy, slightly mashed, rosebud. He presented it to her with a grin. She sighed as if she were mildly exasperated and took it. Inside, she bubbled with pleasure.

"He said you work harder than any human being he's ever known in his life. That they called you the 'child genius.' He said you have the patience of a saint and the ambition of a Rockefeller. That nobody stays at National Health more than two years, but you've been there four."

"I see." She twirled the stem of the rosebud between her fingers and wondered if he'd bought it just for her. Retta placed it on top of her small purse. Later, she'd slip it inside when he wasn't looking. "What else?"

"That's it," he lied. Actually, Burdine had called her "an old-maid type who brushed her teeth after lunch and talked to the plants in the break room," but he wasn't going to repeat that.

"He called me something like 'a mousy old maid,' didn't he?" she asked abruptly. Mac's eyes flew to her face, where he found a mask of dignity but also a touch of amusement. She saw the confirmation in his reaction, and nodded. The waiter brought their drinks and she took a swallow of hers, her movements calm.

Just the facts, sir, just the facts, Mac thought. She was nothing if not straightforward, and that he admired immensely.

"I knew he saw me that way," she added. A wry smile touched her lips. She ran a finger around the rim of her glass, and traced the movement with thoughtful eyes. "The mousy part is true, at least."

"No." She looked up, startled. Mac shook his head slowly, his eyes rebuking. "You're not mousy."

Air refused to travel all the way to her lungs. They shared a quiet gaze. Retta felt as if she'd like to sprout tears, which was ridiculous because all he'd done was compliment her.

"Thank you, Amadeus." She smoothed a hand over the front of her severe suit, wishing abruptly that she'd changed clothes. Changed into what? she asked herself. All she had were suits similar to this one, or simple, unimaginative dresses.

Mac saw the frown that entered her expression. She looked upset, and he felt upset. They'd gotten entirely too serious.

"Tell me something," he said. He mustered every ounce

of teasing cheer he could. "Were you born wearing a business suit, or did you start wearing one in grammar school?"

Her eyes filled with shock at his bold comment, then wavered, then squinted in self-assessment. Finally, a full smile zoomed across her face and she began to laugh. Mac sat, enthralled, and listened to the throaty sound. Underneath this rigid facade lay a gloriously alive human being, and suddenly his chest swelled with a determination to liberate that person.

"Do you say such awful things to your patients?" she demanded breathlessly. "If anyone else said that to me, I'd do something terrible to him. I'm giving you a warning, Dr. Amadeus McHale."

"What would you do?" he wanted to know. Now he looked devilish and unstoppable. "I have a right to know. How does Henrietta P. Stanton react when she gets mad?"

"I . . ." She thought for a moment, then looked defensive. "I clean things. I use constructive outlets for my emotions."

"You clean things?" He looked aghast and amused. "Like what?"

"Oh, my stove, or a closet, or my little car. Once I scrubbed my apartment's kitchen floor with a toothbrush."

"What brought that outrageous behavior on?"

Her eyes darkened and she retreated behind a protective mask. He saw it and pressed forward, nonetheless.

"Talk, now, don't clam up on me. I'm too intrigued."

"I . . ." She looked at him in dismay, hesitating. Oh, what difference did it make? "I had just broken up with someone."

"Oh." Now he looked dismayed. She saw the expression before he replaced it with a neutral one, and her lips parted in a pleased smile. Whatever it really meant, she preferred to assume jealousy had provoked it. A harmless fantasy, this. The man wasn't jealous, of course.

"I dated a fellow I met in college at Northwestern." Retta could hear herself talking too fast, telling details that she would never have offered ordinarily. She felt a compulsion to explain. "We thought it was going to work, but after five years it still hadn't. I ended it."

"How could someone as young as you have had a serious relationship for five years?"

She made a soft sound of offense, and straightened. Her eyes cut into him with somber rebuke.

"I'm twenty-six. That seems young to you, perhaps, but don't patronize me."

"I apologize." Mac ran a hand through his hair in frustration. It wasn't like him to label people. Why was it so difficult to avoid discussing her age? Why did he feel that it was so damned important? "That was an insensitive thing I said."

Her pique collapsed under his sincere, solemn look.

"It's all right; I'm used to it. Almost everyone who works at National Health is under thirty. We're young slave labor. It makes it harder to win the respect and confidence of our sources, and I suppose I understand why."

"No. You've won my respect and confidence already."

She hung on his words with an absurd glow of delight rising inside her. Retta looked down at his hands resting on the table so near hers. He had marvelous hands, big and masculine but graceful. She suddenly wanted to say very unprofessional words of admiration to their owner...

"Aha!"

Startled, she looked up at him. He curled, then uncurled his fingers and produced another rosebud. He winked at her jauntily.

"I knew I had another of these somewhere. Please."

She took it silently, her heart hammering in her throat.

"Your pockets are going to get a rose disease, Mac."

He laughed deeply, but inside he felt desperate to distract both of them from the palpable intensity in the air. Mac deftly flipped her salad fork into his hand and just as deftly made it disappear.

"Give that back," she ordered dryly. "I hope you don't do this sort of thing during surgery."

"It keeps the nurses in stitches."

She groaned at the pun.

"Mac, is this magic hobby of yours a way of relieving stress?"

The fork reappeared from somewhere in the region of his white cuff. He handed it to her with a flourish.

"Yes. And I also practice yoga, and I run. But mostly I play golf."

A disbelieving smile crossed her lips. He winced inwardly, knowing that golf was out of her generational realm.

"What's your handicap?" she asked excitedly. He gave her a puzzled look.

"Four."

"That's great! Mine's ten."

"You play golf, Retta?"

"Almost every day. I'm an addict."

Mac fumbled with his fork, intent on palming it, and dropped it to the floor with uncharacteristic clumsiness. She was perfect. Honest, smart, beautiful, and she played golf. She laughed at his magic gags. She looked at him in a way that made him feel strong and tender and capable of amazing sexual feats.

Oh my God, he thought abruptly. Did I really just imagine what I think I imagined: her serious, delightful face flushed with serious desire, her business suit jettisoned along with whatever businesslike underwear she wore, her naked body waiting for his . . .

"Mac, are you all right?"

"I'm . . . amazed. I thought no one under thirty played golf."

"Well . . ." She looked embarrassed. "Golf isn't all I do. I have other hobbies. I . . . I sew, for instance. I made this suit."

"That's terrific."

He propped his chin on one hand and frowned at her. A paternal attitude would combat his straying thoughts, Mac decided.

Retta shifted uncomfortably in her seat. He seemed to be making a diagnosis about her, and she didn't believe she'd like it. Okay, so I'm not exciting, she thought angrily. I'm hard-working. I pay my bills. I take care of myself without anyone's help. I don't have the time or the inclination to be fluffy and helpless and exciting. I need to break loose. I know it, okay.

"Do you know what you need, Henrietta?" he asked. He sounded stern.

Zoom. Retta felt emotionally naked. Was he a mind reader? "I . . . no . . . what kind of question is that?"

"You need to act your age. You're too young to be so old. Take my advice. Life is too short."

"I'd like to be more like you."

"What?"

Retta gestured at the two rosebuds on her purse. Her voice filled with awe. "You're the youngest person I know. Doing this sleight of hand . . . and . . . the way you laugh. You're forty-two going on twenty-two."

"How did you know that I'm forty-two?"

"I checked your background, remember?" She gazed at him anxiously. "You look perturbed."

"You're categorizing me with those middle-aged men who run around trying to act like college students. I assure you, I'm not in that group."

Retta was stunned for a moment. She leaned forward and her voice came out incredulous. "I didn't mean to insinuate that there's anything wrong with the way you act. You have a lot of *joie de vivre*. I envy you." She paused, looking even more disturbed. "And you're not middle-aged. Good heavens, Mac, is that secretly the way you think of yourself?"

He chuckled, trying to keep the conversation light. "Sometimes."

"Why?"

"Oh," he said lightly, avoiding her eyes, straining to be casual. "I look at men like my friend Vince and pray that nobody thinks I sound like that."

"Like what? A lecher?"

He nodded, smiling. "A lecher."

Retta turned both hands up in a gesture of supplication, then shook her head in disbelief.

"You're not a lecher," she said solemnly.

"I'm not?" Inside, he felt strangely exhilarated. At least they could be friends without her suspecting that he harbored all sorts of feelings toward her—some of them distinctly lecherous. Mac exhaled slowly. "Thank you," he said comically, with exaggerated relief. "I feel so much better now."

"Have I done or said something that makes you feel . . . uncomfortable with me?"

"Not a thing." Liar, he accused himself silently. "I just want you to understand that you have nothing to worry about with me. I'm sure you're used to being hit on by men, but you can relax with yours truly."

"I really appreciate that, Amadeus." Was the man blind? she wondered. Or had he read the interest in her eyes all too easily, and this was his way of diplomatically rejecting her? Retta smiled politely, her best I'm-withering-inside cover-up smile. "Please, Mac. Do some card tricks and let's forget about this strange conversation." Do anything to distract me from wanting to shake you, she added mentally.

Relief stirred inside him. What harm could it do to be her friend? To dedicate the evening to making her laugh? With a calculating smile Mac reached into his jacket. This was safe enough.

"Pick a card," he ordered grandly, as he twirled the deck into a fan. He cocked one brow at her. "Any card."

CHAPTER THREE

"Do it again! Show me, Mac!" the ten-year-old boy at the next table insisted.

Mac grinned, then graciously turned his handkerchief into a dollar bill. Retta smiled. This was the third time the youngster had collected. The kid had brains.

"Give the nice gentleman his money back, Tommy," the boy's mother urged. Tommy's eyes clouded with calculated sorrow. Mac shook his head.

"Keep it." He snatched a quarter from behind the boy's ear and gave that money to him as well. "You've been a good audience."

Mr. and Mrs. Chabot, Tommy's parents, applauded. The Greenburgs, an elderly couple at another nearby table, applauded too, and so did the young couple at the table next to the Greenburgs. All had been treated to Mac's array of skillful magic—both the sleight of hand and the charisma—during the past hour.

Retta sipped her after-dinner coffee and thought for the hundredth time that she couldn't remember when she'd had so much fun. In between discussing the ethics newsletter Mac had managed to make her laugh on a dozen different occasions. He knew great golf jokes.

"I do impressions, too," he'd told her. "Listen. Sylvester Stallone playing Hamlet." He lowered his voice. "Yo. To be or what?"

31

She kept reminding herself that there was nothing unprofessional about having a good time during a business dinner. After all, she had to stay on friendly terms with Mac, didn't she? Newt would want it this way.

"Where to now?" Mac asked her abruptly. He looked at his sturdy wristwatch. With its cloth band and simple dial, it was as unpretentious as he was. "It's only eight-thirty."

"It's a weeknight," she protested without conviction.

"Are you always so responsible, Henrietta?"

She shrugged a little, and didn't answer.

"Aha, I thought so. Well, your common sense and dutiful attitude are hereby recorded. Now, where to?"

She squinted at him as she tried to think.

"We could go to the Pump Room and have a nightcap."

"The Pump Room?" he echoed, and put a hand over his heart in exaggerated shock. "That pinnacle of European elegance? Too stuffy. Let's go roller skating."

"First of all, I don't know how, and second, I won't learn how while wearing a skirt."

"No guts, no glory."

"No. Period." They traded looks of benign challenge. "Are you serious?" she asked. "About roller skating?" She could believe it, from this man.

"Of course. But if you prefer something more tasteful, let's go dancing."

She looked uncertain. "What kind of dancing?"

"Well, I refuse to slam dance, but I'm game for anything else. Could we compromise halfway between punk and ballroom waltzing?"

"How about polka?" she said eagerly. His warm blue eyes widened in slow amusement and surprise.

"You're kidding."

"No, I'm one-fourth Polish."

"What does that mean? That you were born knowing how to polka? Is it genetic?"

She laughed. God, he loved hearing her laugh. Mac felt a surge of pleasure at the way he'd brought her out of her shell during dinner. Two Tom Collinses had helped, because apparently she wasn't much of a drinker. He could tell by the way her face had flushed halfway through the first drink.

"All right, you pick whatever you like, Mac."

"No, polka suits me fine," he said somberly. "But you'll have to teach me how."

"Really, we don't—"

"I want to learn," he interrupted. "Seriously." He had an enormous amount of curiosity about anything new, and he rarely felt bored because of his ability to involve himself with open-minded glee in the world around him.

She caught her lower lip between her teeth and looked at him with gleaming eyes. To be inside the circle of his arms, even during a boisterous polka, would be marvelous.

"We'll have to discuss the newsletter at some point, to make it legit," she warned. "Dancing doesn't fall under Dr. Winston's criteria for entertaining potential advisory board members."

"I wouldn't think of having gratuitous fun during a polka," Mac said gravely. "I doubt I'll have fun at all." His mouth twitched with repressed humor. Retta gave him a wry smile, as if he were an uncontrollable whim she couldn't resist.

"Well, my conscience is clear then. Let's go polka, Amadeus."

A few minutes later they stepped out into the cool, rainy April night amidst the shimmering lights and architectural majesty of Chicago after dark. Retta tugged the collar up on her neat trench coat and eyed him curiously. He wore a bulky, sheepskin coat with heavy white fleece around the collar and the seams.

"You look ready for the mountains," she observed politely. "Do you live in a shepherd's cabin?"

Mac grinned. "I have a condo at Gold Shore. Thirtieth floor. I get snow in July at that altitude. I have to be prepared."

Retta silently considered his address. The Gold Shore Condominiums were expensive and exclusive. They overlooked Lake Michigan, and she'd read in *Chicago* magazine that their prices started at nearly two hundred thousand dollars. He didn't seem like a Gold Shore sort of man. He looked like a . . . a rugged, shepherd's-cabin type. Hmmm.

"You're thinking that I'm a snob," he said cheerfully. They wound their way through a packed parking lot, side-stepping puddles from a recent shower.

Retta gave him a startled look. "I'm just impressed."

"The condo's an investment. And it's close to my office and to the hospital. I used to have a house outside the city, but it just felt too big for one person."

This seemed a good time to casually inquire about his late wife and ask whether he had any children, but she didn't get the chance.

"We'll take my car, okay?" he said. "No sense in both of us driving to that . . . what's the name again?"

"The Starlight Dance Hall."

"The Starlight Dance Hall," he repeated with a touch of irony in his deep voice. "By God, Henrietta, this is going to be different. My car? Okay?"

"Okay."

They walked down an aisle of vehicles and stopped by a low-slung silver contraption.

"Your car?" she said breathlessly.

"Yep. I know how it looks . . ." he said hesitantly.

"Mac, I've never seen a DeLorean before. Not in the flesh—the steel, that is.".

She looked at him with a little concern, as if she'd just discovered a disturbing side to his personality. Mac saw the doubt in her dark eyes.

"It's just an investment," he protested again. *"Medical Economics Magazine* recommended it." She smiled politely. He looked perturbed and uncomfortable. "And . . . oh, all right, Henrietta, I've got a little show-off in me. I admit it."

Her smile warmed. "Confession is good for the soul."

Mac pulled up the gray, winglike passenger door and she slid inside the unique car with a look of intense curiosity on her face. Mac lowered her door and frowned as he walked to the driver's side. He kept intending to get rid of this car, which he'd purchased in a strange, frantic mood after Judith's death. He'd bought the condominium the same way, as if changing his unpretentious habits could change him into someone who didn't hurt so badly.

Retta glanced at the intricate dashboard and found a plastic bag hanging beside the radio. Tentative, a little guilty at being curious, she pulled the open lip back. Mac slid into the driver's seat as she began to laugh—no, to giggle, something she hadn't consciously allowed herself to do in years.

Lollipops. The man carried lollipops and all-day suckers in his DeLorean. He might have a little vanity in him, but he hadn't let it skew his priorities.

"What is it?" he demanded. He followed her line of vision and a self-effacing smile grew on his mouth. "Oh."

"Do you give these to your passengers, Mac?"

"Only when they're very, very good." He pulled a chocolate Tootsie Pop out of the bag for himself. "Please. Help yourself."

So they drove down the glittering city streets in his DeLorean, working away on their lollipops while she considered the complexities of his personality and decided that he was easily the most eccentric man she'd ever met, as well as the sexiest.

The Starlight Dance Hall sat on the outskirts of downtown Chicago in a section that had seen better days. Old row houses and tacky, bright apartment buildings sidled up to the hall, which had originally been home to a grocery store. After berthing the DeLorean between a nondescript sedan and an aging van in the potholed parking lot, Mac walked protectively close to her until they entered the neon-lit hall.

"Great God," he said in amazement. They stopped in the foyer and scanned a dance area that seemed to stretch forever under a high ceiling and multicolored stage lights. "This looks like a retirement home for the Polish national circus."

"Watch it," she warned, although his assessment was offered so gently that it wasn't offensive. And the place did fit his description. The average age of the dancers now trooping around the dance floor to the polka music of a five-piece band was sixty-five.

"Retta, my darling!" a plump-faced grandmother in a bright print dress crooned loudly. She came toward them with open arms, then surrounded Retta in a generous hug. "We have not seen you since we lost Nada. Every Friday night you two would come. Where have you been?"

"I'm sorry," Retta whispered, hugging her back. "It felt too sad to come here alone. I couldn't do it."

"I understand, little one, I do."

Mac studied the embrace with interest and emotion. Retta looked up at him as her friend stepped back.

"Dolores Jankowski, meet Amadeus McHale. You can call him Mac."

Mac cut his eyes at Retta. "No, it's Amadeus," he said somberly, as he took the pink hand Dolores extended. "I'm Austrian." He lifted her hand to his lips and kissed it. She beamed with delight. Retta pressed her lips together to hide a smile. Nothing in his manner suggested that he was making fun of Dolores. No, he was just bringing a touch of magic into her life, as he did for everyone, it seemed.

"Austrian," Dolores repeated in awe. "How wonderful. You must be very good at the waltz."

"Of course."

Retta pursed her lips in rueful consideration of that probable lie. "Come along, Amadeus," she ordered. "We can leave our coats over there near the bar." A pub occupied one corner of the huge hall. Almost as many people came to enjoy its ethnic food and beer as came to dance.

He followed her dutifully. Retta started to shrug off her coat. Suddenly she felt his broad hands on her shoulders. Startled, she turned a blank gaze up at him.

"Oh. Oh, I see," she murmured, as he slipped her coat back.

He frowned in puzzlement. "See what?"

"What you're doing."

Mac cocked one brow at her in mock horror. "Did I violate a dance hall rule? What?"

"I'm just not accustomed to it. Having help with my

coat." She didn't add that the pressure of his hands, even through the material that separated his touch from her skin, was disarmingly provocative.

"I thought you said you were involved with a man for five years."

She nodded. "But he didn't do coats. Or car doors. We agreed that those gestures were outdated and unnecessary."

Mac's hands paused halfway down her arms. He felt like a dinosaur. "Should I stop?"

"No!" She said that a little too fervently. Retta blinked hard, tried to regain her composure, and avoided Mac's quiet gaze.

"I'm older now. The gestures are harmless and I . . . I appreciate them."

Mac frowned as he finished removing her coat and handed it to the rosy-cheeked man who supervised a rack that served as cloak room. He didn't want her to consider him or his gestures harmless. An unrepentant part of his soul wanted to believe that she felt the same powerful attraction he felt.

"Are you all right, Mac?"

He looked down at her to find her hazel eyes locked on his face, scrutinizing him. He cleared his throat and hurriedly concentrated on taking off his coat.

"I'm just terrified of polkas."

She smiled. "Haven't you ever watched Lawrence Welk? They're easy."

"You watch Lawrence Welk?"

"I used to, with Nada. Even in the last months, when she was really . . . sick . . . she enjoyed Lawrence Welk."

Mac touched her arm. His eyes filled with questions. "How long was she ill?"

"Oh . . ." Retta pretended to count, while she strove to make sure her voice remained nonchalant. "Four years."

"You said it was her kidneys?"

"Basically. She thought she had an ordinary kidney infection, but it was nephritis. One thing led to another, and she developed chronic renal failure. Then hypertension from that. In the last month before she died, she had a series of strokes."

"What nursing home was she in?"

"Nursing home?" Retta looked at him with surprise. "She was in the hospital during that last month. Before that, she lived at our apartment."

"You mean you took care of her?"

Retta nodded, and looked at him as if he'd asked a very strange question. "Of course. We couldn't afford outside help. Besides, she was my family. My responsibility. I lived with her and we took care of each other." She couldn't understand the expression of displeasure on his face. "Are you angry about something?"

He realized how he must look, and quickly softened. His fingers tightened on the sleeve of her suit, and Retta's eyes flickered down to them.

"I'm just..." He paused, searching for words. "I'm just thinking that you're a unique and very strong person. And that you must have had a rough time. I wish I could have helped."

"You have," she answered softly. "Just by caring... now."

In the awkward, emotional silence that followed, his hand slipped slowly down her arm to her wrist. By natural progression it touched the back of her hand. To his stunned surprise she turned her palm upward and wound her fingers into his.

Her heart racing, Retta looked down at their joined hands, and he followed. The coarse skin of his big hand and the silky skin of her small one made an erotic contrast —male and female, hard and soft. Without realizing it, they squeezed each other's hands so tightly that the sensation was almost painful. Mac could barely breathe. This was dangerous territory.

"Thank you," he murmured. "You're a sweet girl. I wish I had a daughter like you." Abruptly he brought her hand to his lips and kissed it with a jaunty smack, then let go of it and patted her shoulder.

Surprise and then humiliation filled Retta's eyes. She

hid the emotions quickly, while unhappiness twisted her stomach. What a fool I've been, she thought. I've misinterpreted his kindness and friendship for something else.

"Well," she said gruffly. "I've always thought that the best doctors were father figures."

She couldn't have depressed him more if she'd called him "Gramps" and asked how late he could stay out before he began to get sleepy.

"Are you going to teach me to dance?" he asked abruptly, seeking any way to distract his jumbled emotions. Mac forced a smile. "Tomorrow is a work day, and we both have to get home."

"Yes." Her face rigidly composed, she led the way to the dance floor.

The band had recently begun a slow waltz. In the midst of the crowded hall Retta simply stopped, turned around to face Mac, and held up both hands without much enthusiasm. He grasped them with just as little excitement, feeling tense and miserable.

"I know how to do this," he told her. "I can waltz in my sleep."

"If you can waltz, you can polka."

"I only polka in my nightmares."

She smiled faintly and tried to ignore the feel of his strong hands pressing around hers. He brought one of her hands to his chest and held it against the rough houndstooth of his jacket. They kept their bodies several inches apart and managed to look everywhere but into each other's eyes.

He did waltz well, she admitted, even for a man with such long legs. It would have been so lovely to snuggle close to his tall body and place her head on his shoulder. She estimated that he was six-one or six-two.

"So," Mac said casually. "Tell papa about this young whippersnapper who never helped you with your coat or your car door."

"That about sums it up." The last thing she wanted was to think about any other man right now.

"You said earlier that you met him in college."

Retta sighed at his persistence. "We met as freshmen at Northwestern. His name's Jay Monroe. He's an advertising rep now, in New York."

"Did he have honorable intentions?"

"Yes. And he could charm the butterflies off the flowers, despite that stuff about coats and cars. He still can. He's adorable."

"How interesting." Mac allowed himself the luxury of a sardonic, jealous expression. Because she refused to look at him—which bothered him more and more as the waltz continued—he had the privacy to grimace and frown. "Why did you let him get away?"

"He never grew up." His puzzled silence asked for more information. "He was a victim of the Peter Pan syndrome. A perpetual little boy. I finally realized that I was playing mommy, running after him, doing his laundry, loaning him money—taking care of him when I barely had time to take care of myself and work and look after Desinada."

"Was there a time when you wanted to marry him?"

"Yes. But by the time he started to mature a little and decided that he wanted to get married, too, I'd been too bruised by his wishy-washy attitude. We never wanted the same thing at the same time."

"You broke it up?"

"Yes. Two years ago."

"And you made up for lost time, I hope." He didn't hope that at all, but he was trying to say the right damned words.

"Sure." She didn't sound very convincing. Mac looked down at her skeptically. She let her gaze touch him, skitter away with a hint of chagrin, then return. "I spend a lot of time on my career." She sounded defensive. "I don't have much time to date anybody." Her voice dropped. "And you see, Nada died not long after Jay and I quit seeing each other, so I just haven't felt sociable."

"That was what? Two years ago? You're too young to be working so hard and enjoying life so little."

"Youth has nothing to do with it. You work hard and appear to enjoy life a lot."

"Oh. And I'm not young, I see," he teased.

"Dammit." She stopped moving, which forced him to stop as well. Mac looked down into her angry eyes—their hazel background now full of sparks—and saw a new side of her. She glared up at him. "I didn't mean it that way. You are young."

"Don't talk to your elders in that tone of voice."

"Don't treat me like a child, Dr. McHale."

"Come here and be quiet."

He pulled her close to him, and she gasped. With her head tilted back, her face inches from his, Retta gazed numbly into his blue eyes and the lean handsomeness of his features.

"Waltz," she ordered. She didn't know what else to say. Everything seemed to be getting confused.

"Yes, ma'am."

Now they waltzed the way two people were supposed to—close, with his cheek resting against her forehead. Unfortunately, the song ended thirty seconds later. But by then Retta was trembling from the contact with his body, and his senses had concentrated all their attention on the delicate scent of her hair and the smooth texture of her brow against his chin.

"Oh boy, now we're gonna do some polka tunes!" the band leader announced, sounding just like Lawrence Welk.

"Oh, God," Mac groaned.

"Follow my lead," she urged. "It's really simple. You're a good dancer, so you'll catch it quickly."

"I wish I'd been vaccinated. I don't think I want to catch it."

Despite all his jokes, he easily learned the rhythm. After a little fumbling he was able to guide them both with a semblance of dignity during the first dance. He improved in the second, and by the third he started grinning and humming.

"Fantastic!" The tune bounced to a stop and he spun Retta in a circle. Mac got so caught up in watching her glossy hair turn from prim style into a sexy tumble of brown waves that he let go of her hand too soon and she stumbled.

Mac caught her in a heap of gray business suit and startled hazel eyes, and she latched onto his shoulders from pure instinct.

"Be careful," she quipped breathlessly. "Polkas can be dangerous."

"I know," he said just as breathlessly. They stared at each other for a moment, on the verge of something wild and impulsive. Retta slipped a hand up to his face and brushed a wisp of gold-gray hair back into place at his temple. Her fingertips lingered against his cheek.

Abruptly he stepped back, his eyes troubled. She read his displeased expression and winced.

"That wasn't very professional of me, McHale. I guess . . . I think of you as a friend. I was too casual, though. Sorry."

He still looked upset. But now his mouth gentled into a smile that was reassuring but somehow very sad.

"I want you to think of me that way," he told her softly.

Retta nodded slowly. Inside, she burned with regret. "Terrific," she murmured, and smiled.

"That's it for tonight, folks," the band leader said over a raspy microphone. "Join us Friday night until one A.M. But now the old clock on the wall says it's ten o'clock and that's bye-bye time on Wednesdays."

"Bye-bye time?" Mac repeated with more amusement than he felt. "And I was just getting into it."

He slid a hand under her elbow and they headed toward the coat rack.

"If you ever feel the need to polka, just let me know," she offered. "And . . . if you want to bring a . . . friend here sometime, you remember how to find the place, don't you?"

"I have no friends," he said with a deep sigh.

"Right, McHale. The passenger seat of that DeLorean was specially designed to carry beautiful women in slinky evening gowns."

"Well, some night you put on a slinky business suit and we'll polka up a storm."

She smiled broadly as he helped her with her coat.

The ride back to the parking lot at Barney's took only fifteen minutes. As he wheeled the DeLorean into a space she sat bolt upright.

"The one thing I haven't done tonight is get your answer about the newsletter!" She looked at him in quiet desperation. Newt would be furious. "Have you made a decision yet?"

Mac fiddled with his key ring, pretending to straighten errant keys on it, while he tried to be logical. The smart tactic would be to refuse her request. That way, he wouldn't have to see her again, wouldn't have to feel torn between his sense of dignity and his overwhelming attraction to a woman sixteen years his junior.

Men had romances with much younger women all the time, and he knew he was an oddity. But his feelings were regimented by convictions he couldn't ignore.

"Tell old Newt," he said slowly, his eyes on the key ring, "that I'm very interested. That our discussion was very positive. But I need to look at my schedule and think about it."

"I know the money we're offering is just a token," she said lamely. He had to take the offer. How else would she have an excuse to see him? "But I'd make certain that your commitment was minimal. You wouldn't be tied to any detailed duties just because you head the advisory board."

"Let me think about it," he repeated. Mac smiled at her gently. "I know it means a lot to you." He paused, intent on hiding his real reasons for stalling. "I'll make a list of my questions and concerns."

"I'll buy you another dinner, or lunch, and we can talk about them." Retta knew she sounded too eager. "Or . . . I can give you a call. Whatever."

He frowned dramatically. "We need to talk in person. I won't have to polka next time, will I?"

She laughed, almost weak with relief. "No."

"Good. Meet me Saturday morning and we'll play golf."

"That would be great, Mac!"

He knew he was being greedy, but he couldn't help himself. "Park Lakes Country Club. Get over there about eight and we'll have breakfast first."

"I know where it is. I'll be there." The ritzy suburban club was a far cry from the cheap public courses she used. But that was beside the point. She didn't care where they met, or why, as long as she saw him again.

"Come on, Henrietta. I'll walk you to your car."

"Oh, you don't have to . . ."

Mac pushed his door up, then looked back over his shoulder with a rebuking gaze. "Don't tell me Peter Pan talked you into handling your own coat, opening your own doors, *and* protecting yourself in city parking lots at night. That young man had a good thing going."

With that remark he got out and walked to her side. Retta nearly purred with the simple pleasure of having this kind of attention from Mac, even if it was just a gentlemanly gesture. She stepped out of the DeLorean and he closed the door.

"You said you drive a . . ." he paused, trying to remember.

"Ford Escort." She pointed to the small, dark-blue car and they headed toward it.

"Great God, what do you do? Polish it with a toothbrush? I've never seen such a perfect wax job."

"I told you that cleaning things is one of my hobbies."

They stopped by the car and she searched in her purse for a moment until she located her keys.

"I'm set," she said and held them up. If he would just walk away now she knew she could keep herself from saying or doing anything unseemly. "Thanks for the protection."

He nodded, but didn't leave. His eyes were serious—too serious. Too tempting.

"Retta, I just want you to know that I had a fantastic

time tonight. You're a helluva lady." With that he held out his hand. "I look forward to talking to you again."

She stared at his hand. Retta felt cross signals between them. He was formal, but he was provocative. He was retreating, but advancing at the same time. He used humor to hide a very intense nature. She slid her hand into his and squeezed slowly.

The contact made her throat close and fingers of sensation scattered down her spine. Her eyes rose up his torso until they reached his face. What she saw there confirmed her best hope.

"Mac," she whispered joyfully. And before he knew what she intended, she leaned upward and brushed a kiss across his mouth. Retta wavered for a second, ready to step back.

Through his hand she felt a shiver like a small earthquake. Her eyelids half-closed, she dared to meet his gaze. It burned her to the core with desire.

"This is foolish," he murmured hoarsely. Then he pulled her to him and sank his mouth onto hers.

She cried out with pure pleasure as his kiss proved even more magnificent than she'd imagined. He had a generous mouth, firm and sensual. They kissed roughly for several seconds, their mouths open but innocent. Then his arms wrapped her tighter against his chest.

His tongue touched hers gently. The nature of the kiss became slow, hypnotizing as she met it with her own. The kiss stopped suddenly, but their mouths remained close, their ragged breaths mingling.

"That was the wrong thing for friends to do," he managed eventually.

"Oh, really." She thought he was teasing, and she started to touch her mouth to his again. His hands slid to her shoulders and held her away.

"No."

Retta looked at him with dawning disbelief. No man kissed like that for friendship's sake. In fact, she'd never been kissed so sensually before.

"What's wrong, Mac?"

"I don't understand why you did that."

"I . . . I wanted to kiss you. I thought you wanted me to kiss you."

He nearly groaned out loud. Somewhere deep inside he reveled in the sweet, sweet knowledge that he'd been wrong—this lovely woman didn't consider him a father figure. At the same time, he couldn't allow himself to get involved with her.

Retta analyzed the regret in his expression and drew the only conclusion she could. Her heart sank.

"Oh, Mac, I shouldn't have done that," she bluffed. "It was just an impulse, horribly unprofessional, and . . ."

"Sshh." He shook his head and smiled wearily. "Just don't do it again. I kissed you back because you caught me off guard. But I won't do it again."

She ached as if he'd struck her. "I understand," she murmured. Retta felt as if pins were sticking into her stomach. Still, she managed to remain calm on the surface. "You . . . if you want someone else from National Health to work with you . . ."

"No." Bastard, he rebuked himself. He ought to say yes, but he couldn't. He looked at her from under his brows, trying to appear calm and very wise while underneath his emotions churned without any organization at all. "I think we've settled the misunderstanding, haven't we?"

"Yes," she murmured. Humiliation made her face burn.

"Don't," he said quickly. "Don't feel bad." He squeezed her shoulders and let go, then stepped back. "Remember, we are friends. Good friends, even though we've just met. That's a very special bond to form so soon."

"Yes," she echoed, and smiled. Oh God, just make him quit talking and leave me alone. Retta managed to laugh. "You see what happens after a night of polka? I lost my control for a minute." She unlocked her car door and numbly pulled it open.

He smiled, but his eyes searched her face anxiously. "Start your car," he said softly. "I'll wait just to make sure it's all right."

Tears caught in her throat. Still smiling calmly, Retta

settled in the driver's seat. She rolled down her window with one hand and slid the key into the car's ignition with the other. She felt grateful when the soft hum of the engine formed a background noise that interfered with the tension in the air.

"Saturday?" she asked. "Do you still think it's a good idea? I'll understand . . ."

"Saturday." He pointed at her in mild warning. "You be there."

"All right." God, I can't believe I'm handling this so easily, she thought. She knew that as soon as she could, she'd cry. And then she'd clean. Or sew. Possibly all night.

"Good night, Henrietta." She absorbed the wistful but determined humor in his voice. Whatever he wanted from her, she knew she'd give it to him.

"Good night, Amadeus." She touched a finger to her forehead in a tiny salute, and drove away.

Mac shoved his hands into his slacks pockets and strained his eyes to watch her car until it disappeared into the night. He felt ancient and alone.

CHAPTER FOUR

RETTA DIDN'T KNOW how to deal with luxury. She recognized her nervousness and smiled sardonically as she nosed her unassuming little car through the massive stone gates set with bronze plaques proclaiming "PARK LAKES COUNTRY CLUB. ESTABLISHED 1947. PRIVATE."

The lush grounds draped in early spring greenery only prompted her to think of the cramped old apartment she and Desinada had shared and all the meager years when they'd saved every extra penny.

"Nada, I wish you could see where your little girl is today," Retta murmured as she guided her car between rows of manicured shrubs. She tried to roll the tension out of her shoulders, tried to think of anything but the prospect of seing Mac again.

Retta's mouth grew hard. Nada had taught her pride and independence and diligence. She could and would deal with this elusive man simply by refusing to think about him in a personal way anymore.

Nada, who loved flowers, had often called her "an old-fashioned iris." Sturdy. A survivor. Well, I may not bloom around Mac McHale, but I'll never wilt, she thought tautly.

"Good grief, this place is huge," she said out loud as the sprawling, L-shaped clubhouse came into view. It curved through a stand of old oaks glimmering with dew in the early morning sun. The building was majestic, festooned with ornate white cornices that contrasted against the rugged stone of the walls.

Retta parked across from a canopied walkway that led to a stone archway, which in turn led to massive oak doors. With her ancient golf bag weighing down one shoulder and a tote bag dragging at the opposite hand, she lumbered up the walkway and into a cool foyer that was light and modern in design.

"I'm here to meet Dr. Bronson McHale," she told a dignified man wearing a white golf shirt and perfectly pressed white shorts. A badge identified him as the assistant manager. "For breakfast. But I'm a little early."

A teenage boy, also dressed in an immaculate white shorts set and also wearing a name badge, appeared soundlessly from a room designated "club check-in."

"Wow, clubs from the Egyptian tombs," he observed. He took them and her tote bag.

"Be careful with that golf bag," Retta urged dryly. "The Smithsonian has a claim on it when I die."

"Please," the assistant manager said. He gestured to a bright, open hallway that led back into the building. "Follow me to the club restaurant. I'll tell Dr. McHale to meet you there."

The restaurant took her breath away. Sunlight streamed in from a whole wall of windows that overlooked the eighteenth green of the championship golf course.

Although a number of early-morning golfers sat at indoor tables, most were enjoying breakfast at tables under pastel umbrellas on a white deck outside the windows. Retta noted that linen and crystal were in evidence even on the outdoor tables. Intimidation took seed inside her stomach.

"Juice?" a waiter offered immediately after the maître d' had seated her outside.

"Thank you."

She sipped her drink, fervently wishing she'd stayed at home. The people seated around her were elegant and well heeled in a casual way that said they were comfortable being comfortable. She didn't belong here.

"Henrietta!"

She turned at the rich sound of an unmistakable voice, looking up at Mac striding toward her, then did a double take. Knickers. The man was wearing knickers and plaid socks.

People stared, smiled, and shook their heads benignly as if they expected him to be outrageous. He carried himself with confidence, and he made a striking, if bizarre, entrance. Retta leaned her chin on one hand and sighed.

"Good morning, Amadeus," she said. The dull ache inside her wanted to grow, but she ignored it.

"How are you, Retta?"

Mac said that with too much concern and too much pain as he gazed down at her. He cautioned himself to be less obvious. But she looked lovely and very proper to him, her back rigid, one leg crossed delicately over the other, her sturdy chin thrust forward almost in defiance of the awkwardness between them.

"I'm very fine," she lied.

"And you look it." That was no lie. Mac stuck his hand out and she shook it briefly, firmly, but let go and pulled away first. "Henrietta, why are you looking at me as if I have tentacles and scales?"

"Your outfit." Besides the fact that her heart had done unnatural gymnastics when he'd called her name, she was shaken up by his choice of golf clothes. Retta couldn't help chuckling.

He looked down at himself as he lowered his body into the chair across from her. Mac nodded. "What's wrong with blue knickers? I'm wearing this nice striped golf shirt that matches them, so it's not like my colors are uncoordinated. Besides, knickers are Scottish, and golf was invented in Scotland. I'm being traditional."

"It's the plaid knee socks and running shoes that add such an eccentric touch."

"The socks'll look fine with my golf shoes."

"I've been sitting here thinking how formal and stuffy this place is, and you just destroyed my illusions, Doctor."

He nodded, smiling too broadly, he knew, but trying

just as hard as she was to make superficial chitchat as if they hadn't shared a world-stopping encounter three days ago. Mac propped his elbows on the table and accepted orange juice from the waiter. He tilted the glass toward her in a salute.

"Groucho Marx said he didn't want to belong to any club that'd have a guy like him for a member. Somebody has to give these folks something to be appalled at." He paused, his summer-blue eyes scanning her. "But you, on the other hand, fit in nicely."

Retta shifted, then focused her attention on a remnant of orange juice in her glass. She felt his eyes absorb every detail of her tailored white slacks, yellow sports shirt, and thin white sweater. It was hard to think. The man looked fantastic, even in those strange knickers. They outlined the long, taut shape of thighs that should have belonged to an Olympic runner.

"Were you all right?" he asked abruptly. His voice had dropped to a low, throaty level. Retta jerked her eyes up, startled.

"The other night? Certainly. I was embarrassed, that's all."

"Nothing to be embarrassed about."

Didn't he know when to just shut up and sit there? Wasn't it bad enough that the golf shirt revealed a muscular, trim torso and the intriguing pattern of dark brown hair on his long arms? And that even after her humiliation she could barely keep from being hypnotized by his endearing voice and soul-warming smile?

"Good," she said swiftly. "But if Dr. Winston ever hears about it, he'll have a fit."

Mac cocked one sandy brown brow at her. "You think I'd mention it to him?" His voice was reproachful.

"I apologize." She looked at him with self-rebuke in her eyes. "Let's just forget it happened, all right? Believe me, I've never leapt upon a business acquaintance before, and I'll never do it again."

He chuckled, but his eyes were unhappy. "All right," he

said slowly. They sat there in strained silence for a moment. "Are you hungry?"

She gave him an apologetic look. "No. I don't eat breakfast. But you go ahead."

"And I bet you don't take vitamins or get enough sleep. You should eat breakfast."

She made a disgruntled sound of exasperation. He has sharp intuition about my lifestyle, Retta admitted silently.

"I'm too busy most mornings."

"Between seeing patients at my office and running to Rush-Presbyterian to make rounds I hardly sit down some days. But I always eat breakfast."

"Very commendable, Dr. McHale. I bet your idea of breakfast consists of a Tootsie Pop and a glass of milk."

"Well . . ." He stopped, flabbergasted. Bingo. She saw the admission in his face and he looked so comically undone that she burst into soft laughter. He put one hand on his lean hip and squinted at her in mock anger. God, she reads my mind, he thought. It was unnerving.

"Let's go play a round of golf," Mac ordered. She nodded, looking pleased with herself for shocking him.

"If you win, I'll buy you a whole bag of suckers," Retta promised. "But you won't win."

"Henrietta, I'll win, I'll claim my suckers, and I'll tell the other members that you're a polka addict. You'll be ruined."

"I like challenges," she replied tartly. He stood, she stood, and they shared a look that simmered with deep affection. Both of them made uncertain movements. Retta turned her gaze away from him, frowning. "Which way do we go to get to the locker areas? The attendant who took my antique golf bag looked disgusted—like he might be planning to donate it to the Salvation Army. I have to rescue my mother's clubs."

"That way," Mac said, smiling. He pointed to an exit inside the dining room. "Go ahead. I'll tell the waiter we're leaving."

Retta started winding her way through the crowded tables. Mac watched the swing of her compact, athletic body, admiring curves that had been hidden by the business suit, his eyes wistful. Distracted, he held up a hand to catch the waiter's attention.

"McHale!"

Mac swung his gaze around to find a dapper little man grinning up at him slyly.

"Hello, Allen." Allen Dewberry, proctologist, had beautiful white hair, grandchildren, and a new wife who'd just turned twenty-seven.

"I don't believe it, McHale. Have you finally got yourself a young lady friend?"

"She's a medical editor. We have business to discuss."

"The cozy way you two were looking at each other, I'd say she'd like to discuss something else."

Mac's jaw tightened. "I prefer my wine with a little more vintage to it," he said slowly. "You prefer grapes."

Allen only grinned wider, and winked. "Grapes are just a very fine wine waiting to happen." He slapped Mac's shoulder. "You old son of a gun. I knew you had some devil in you. She's a great-looking gal."

Chortling, he walked back to a table full of men. Mac felt embarrassment surge inside his chest. The waiter walked up, and Mac eyed him distractedly. Then a mischievous smile crossed his face.

"Put the juice on my tab. Here. For your trouble." He handed the young man a ten-dollar bill. "Has Dr. Dewberry had his juice yet?"

"No, sir."

"Good. Take him a bowl of oranges and an empty glass."

"Yes, sir!"

Whistling, Mac sank his hands in his knicker pockets and ambled away.

"Great God! What a swing!"

Retta watched her shot bounce neatly as it hit the fairway. The surprise—and, more important, the pride—in Mac's voice made her knees weak with pleasure. She let the shank of her club rest jauntily on her shoulder and shrugged.

"It's a little short. I play stronger on the city courses, but that's because I'm . . ." She started to say "less distracted," but that would give her away. ". . . I'm, uh, a better player in the afternoons than in the morning. I play after work."

"Remind me never to play golf with you in the afternoon," he teased.

"You're beating me by fifteen strokes and we're on the eighteenth hole, so you've got nothing to worry about. Looks like I'm going to be the one to fork over a bag of Tootsie Pops."

They gathered their clubs and started down the fairway, their golf shoes making squishy sounds in the thick grass. He glanced over at her, marveling at the way she managed to perspire but still look appealing and rigidly neat.

"I'm glad you don't like to rent a cart," she noted suddenly.

"I was afraid you thought I'm a scrooge. I just like the exercise."

"I do, too."

They walked along in silence for a moment. "You do everything with such enthusiasm," she murmured.

"That's a real polite way of saying that I sweat a lot."

She turned eyes that gleamed with amusement toward him. "No. You know how to lose yourself in whatever you do. I envy you."

"Life is too short. Live while you can." He paused, then smiled in a self-deprecating way. "Want to hear my other clichés?"

"Have you always been this upbeat and clichéd?"

"No."

Retta took a deep breath. "I read that your wife died of leukemia a few years ago. Life must not have been very happy for you."

He walked a little faster, and she had to hurry to keep up with his long strides. Retta glanced anxiously at his profile, but found no hint of anger in his straight, lean features, only thoughtfulness.

"It was a bad time for everyone who loved her."

"Do you have any children?"

"Yep. A son. Lucas. He's in school at Northwestern. He's got his mother's Norwegian blond good looks, and he's a great guy. He's coming home tonight and we're going to a Cubs pre-season game."

"How old is he?"

"Twenty-one." An awkward second preceded his next words. "You two would get along well."

"Ah, younger men," she said in exaggerated appreciation, a little annoyed. "Pretty to look at, but too immature. I'd be embarrassed."

Mac stopped abruptly, his mouth open. "He's only five years younger than you . . ." His voice trailed off as he realized the subtle trap she was setting. Mac cocked a brow at her and gave her a rebuking look. "I never said you were immature."

"But you are embarrassed to be seen with me."

Retta pulled her golf bag higher onto her shoulder and trudged onward, her mouth set in a grim line. *There. I said what's been in the back of my mind since Wednesday night.*

He caught up with her in two long strides. "'Embarrassed' is not the right word, Retta. Any man would be proud to have you by his side."

Something odd and poignant stirred under her rib cage, and goose bumps ran up her arms.

"Any man my own age, you mean." She stopped again, and looked at him with wistful eyes. "Is that what was wrong the other night? You think I'm too young?" Retta swallowed hard. "Or is it just that I misjudged what I saw in your eyes? Or that you have a commitment to someone else? If you . . . if you'd tell me the reason why you said 'This is foolish' before you kissed me, I'd feel a lot better. And I'll never mention the subject again. I swear."

He looked down at her with distraught eyes. She lived

by the truth, demanded it. Her straightforward attitude and frankness told him that.

"All right," Mac said softly. "I'm very attracted to you. Very," he emphasized. "But I don't like the age difference between us."

Happiness zoomed through Retta and lit her face with a wide smile. He studied it pensively, his heart catching.

"I'm not just being noble," he told her. "I mean it. I'm not going to be some old man doddering after young women."

"Amadeus McHale, forty-two is not old! And I'm not a baby!" She laughed. He couldn't be serious. Sixteen years' difference meant nothing. "Older men get involved with younger women all the time!"

"And it sounds glamorous when it's two celebrities and you read about it in *People* magazine. But nobody interviews them years later when she's bringing him his teeth each morning and buying new batteries for his hearing aid."

Retta frowned. Her mouth popped open in disbelief. "If you were fifty and I was eighteen I might understand this morbid notion of yours. But you're not that much older than I am. Besides, I'm the old one in this pair. When I'm with you I feel ancient because you're so vibrant."

"That's just the hum from my pacemaker," he quipped.

"Mac!" she rebuked. They started walking again, Mac's gaze fixed straight ahead with determination, as Retta twisted her body sideways to stare up at him. "Was your wife the same age as you?"

"Yes. We met in college and got married when we were twenty."

"Have you been dating women your own age since . . . for the past few years?"

"I don't date much."

"Why not?" They reached her golf ball and stopped.

"You're very blunt, Retta. I'm intimidated," Mac said drolly.

"It's the old reporter in me. Why not?"

Mac considered telling her the truth, but decided it

would sound too melodramtic and evoke nothing but sympathy from her. Watching his lovely, loving Judith sink into bedridden dependency maintained by useless and cruel medical technology had nearly driven him crazy.

Out of his bitterness and frustration had come the knowledge that he would never, ever let anyone suffer for him as he had suffered for her. He'd never risk becoming a burden to anyone. He'd remain alone. Mac jerked a thumb toward the neat white sphere buried in the grass.

"A seven iron ought to do the job."

"I'm going to threaten you with one if you don't answer my question." She slid her golf bag to the ground and crossed her arms over her chest defiantly. He frowned.

"After eighteen years of marriage I didn't fit into the singles scene very well." That was another reason he preferred to be alone, he admitted.

She stood there, looking at the most outgoing, most attractive man she'd ever met and shook her head in bewilderment. "What do you mean?"

Mac looked at the sky. He looked at the ground. He slid his hands inside his pockets and pursed his mouth in a concentrated effort to form a good lie. Nothing worked. He did not intend to be the kind of man who chased young women as if they were a magic elixir that stopped time.

"I went out a few times. I tried damned hard to do what seemed normal. But in eighteen years somebody had changed a lot of the rules of dating and forgotten to tell me. I felt like Rip Van Winkle—only Rip never had to contend with sex toys, one-night stands, social diseases, and cynical women out to prove they could use him before he used them."

Retta looked at him with a rush of tenderness. He had a very vulnerable side to him, and she could hear it now in the wistful way he spoke.

"Mac," she said gently. "I want you to know that we're not all like that."

"I know." He cleared his throat. "Are you going to take your shot or not?" Mac looked at the clubhouse sitting at the end of the fairway, just beyond the green. The deck was crowded with the Saturday brunch crowd. "Don't over-shoot and hit somebody in the cocktail."

"Are you going to keep treating me like your daughter? That was a fantastic moment we shared Wednesday night, Amadeus, and I think you'd like to repeat it. I know I would."

"What happened to your promise never to leap on a business acquaintance again?"

"Mac, if you don't quit bluffing . . ."

"I'm not bluffing. I intend to think of you as a daughter." He looked at her sternly.

"I won't let you."

"A cranky, stubborn daughter."

"Are you going to give me an answer about the editorial advisory board?"

"Yes. The answer's no. I don't think it'd be wise for us to work together." Anger colored his expression now. This had gone beyond teasing. They had to get some things straight. "Unless we can keep this relationship on a purely platonic level. I mean what I say, Retta. By God, I do. I'll accept the offer if you promise not to expect anything but a business relationship."

Retta's expression faded from disbelief to shock. Her eyes widened and bright dots of pink formed on her cheeks. She reached down and snatched up her golf ball.

"That's blackmail."

"I know." He shouldered his bag and walked a few yards forward to retrieve his own golf ball. "Come on. Let's get a sandwich and discuss the advisory board. I know it's important to you."

He walked toward the eighteenth green, leaving her standing still, staring after him in stunned anger. So he thought he could manipulate her, did he? He thought he could hide behind his work and his facade of carefree humor?

Well, he had a lot to learn about her, then. *I have a lot to learn about myself,* Retta added, *because I can't believe I'm going to do what I'm about to do.*

Retta stalked after him, reckless and single-minded. He

reached the green, set his bag down, and began to jerk protective covers over each of his clubs. She walked up behind him and dropped her bag with a rattling thud.

"McHale, you coward." He turned around, astonished. "You make such a grand show of being alive, but you're not."

He smiled grimly. "Retta, I can be real stubborn . . ."

His voice trailed away as she stepped up to him and slid her arms around his neck. Retta looked up at the clubhouse deck. Curious club members looked back.

"I'm going to blow your cover," she said tautly, and kissed him with a wanton, open mouth.

Mac made a strangled sound of protest, then a softer sound of reproach, then just a soft sound. His hands clasped her waist and he delved into her sweetness without intending to, his brain buzzing with No—yes—why not? *Dear God, she's fantastic.*

Reason returned quickly, and in the midst of the kiss he reached up, grabbed her wrists, and firmly pulled her arms off his neck. She stepped back, and he saw no victory in her expression, only regret.

"I can't work with you under the conditions you offer, Dr. McHale," she said. Her voice was sad and sardonic. "If you think it's best, we can say good-bye right now."

Mac took a deep breath. *Let her go,* he commanded himself silently.

"Then it's good-bye." His voice was husky but firm.

Retta nodded, her eyes glittering with tears she'd never allow to fall. She picked up her golf bag and walked away.

CHAPTER FIVE

"I WANT MORE commas in this copy! I want shorter sentences! I want more lists! Short. Short. Instructional. Just like the articles in *Popular Mechanics!*"

"What?" Retta and Vanessa chorused. Retta looked at Vanessa and they shared a puzzled frown before looking up at the executive editor in confusion. Scott sat to one side, his stalwart chin buried in one hand.

"Popular Mechanics?" Scott repeated wryly. "You mean like 'Build a better kidney in three easy steps'? or maybe, 'Prostate projects you can finish in one afternoon'?"

"Yes!" Hilda Grimes—as thin as mountain air and twice as cold-natured—peered at them over ugly brown glasses and toyed with her limp blond hair. Retta had always thought she looked like a neo-Nazi librarian. "When the circulation figures go down, we have to find out why," Hilda continued. "We're obviously not catching the readers' attention."

"But Hilda, if the newsletters have lost a few subscribers it's because the promotions have been late, and that's not our fault," Retta protested.

"I can't tell the editors in my group to use more commas," Vanessa said wistfully. She pushed her black hair back and held the sides of her delicate face as if cracks might appear at any minute. "Last week it was fewer charts. The week before that it was longer paragraphs. Now it's shorter sentences and more lists? What do you want? Short sentences with lots of commas in long paragraphs with lists?"

"Yes," Hilda snapped. Her phone rang. "That's all. Excuse me."

Retta followed Scott and Vanessa into the hall and shut Hilda's door behind them.

"All right, youse guys," Scott intoned in his best Jimmy Cagney voice, "it's time to take over dis joint and bust out. The warden's a scab. Are you wid me or against me?"

Retta smiled wearily and reached up to pat his shoulder. Tall, lanky, and easy-going, Scott reminded her of Mac. Her throat ached with sadness. Just two days ago she'd said good-bye to a man she hardly knew, and yet she missed him dreadfully.

"This, too, shall pass," she told Scott—and herself.

"My boards!" someone screamed around a corner somewhere. "Newt got hold of my final copy before it went to the printer, and he's changing everything! I'll never make my deadline now!" They heard a long "Auuuugggh," followed by the sound of a head thumping rhythmically against a wall.

"I better go see about Bob," Vanessa said weakly and left.

"Retta Stanton call extension twenty-five," the receptionist ordered over the hall intercom. "It's urgent."

"Newt wants you right away, my pretty," Scott said fiendishly. "It's been nice working with you, Ms. Stanton." He squeezed her hand in mute sympathy.

Newt Winston sat behind his sleek rosewood desk in his sleek, designer-mauve office and looked out at her from under eyebrows that resembled two red caterpillars trying to kiss. His graying red hair was ruffled. His monogrammed shirt was rumpled. His expression was limply perturbed. He always made Retta think of sugary pink breakfast cereal—soggy underneath and only palatable in small amounts.

"I can't have this kind of behavior," he chastized somberly, thumping his manicured nails on his desk pad. "When you make soup, you don't have to stir with your hands."

Retta squared her shoulders proudly. Inside, she rapidly calculated that she could survive precisely one month on her savings while she looked for another job.

"I'm sorry your friend saw me kiss Dr. McHale on Saturday," she said sincerely. "But I don't think an incident that happens on a weekend, on my own time, is of any importance to National Health."

"We're putting together a very fine soup for this ethics newsletter," Newt continued, unheeding. "With the best ingredients. Now if the chef mishandles one of those ingredients, how can we be sure the soup will win awards?"

The bizarre analogy left her silent. She wanted to laugh, more from misery than anything else, and she dug her nails into her palms to stay calm.

"I apologize," Retta muttered.

"Dr. Winston?" the receptionist said over the phone intercom. "Pardon, but is Retta in your office right now?"

"Yes."

They both heard someone talking in the background. Then the receptionist said, "But you can't . . . wait . . ." and gasped a barnyard obscenity that made Newt blush. Whoever had provoked her ire didn't have far to go to reach Retta, because Newt's office was near the front entrance and reception area. A hand rapped loudly at the office door.

"Yes?" Newt said in stentorian tones.

The heavy door swung open and Mac stepped into the room. Retta could feel the shock spreading across her face while her body automatically came to attention. Her lips parted in surprise.

Mac's eyes sought hers and he winked. "Good morning, Henrietta, you look very, very nice on this fine Monday."

"Good morning, Dr. McHale," she said with a blank nod. He looked perfectly magnificent in a tweed jacket, a gray sweater vest, and black trousers. The knot of a black

tie peaked over the vest. He looked like a man in charge of
the situation.

"Dr. McHale!" Newt boomed. He scurried around his
desk and held out a pink hand. Mac shook it, and she
noticed that his hail-fellow-well-met grip made Newt blink
swiftly and retreat back behind his desk. "Please, have a
seat! What can I do for you?"

Mac didn't answer. He turned to Retta and offered his
hand. She gazed up into his eyes and found apology and
sorrow there. The back of her throat felt scratchy and she
smiled as she grasped his hand for a quick shake. Mac
looked at Newt, then nodded toward Retta.

"My golf partner. I understand there's some problem
with her dedication to duty?"

"Er, yes," Newt muttered, and slumped down in his
chair. He didn't like confrontation. Mac gave her a reassuring look and sat down in the plush guest chair next to
hers. He crossed his long legs, clasped his hands together
in his lap, and completed the impression of being totally at
ease by swinging one loafered foot.

"Well, there shouldn't be," Mac told him cheerfully. "I
told her she'd have to kiss me before I'd agree to join the
advisory board. That's the only reason she embarrassed
herself in front of everyone in the clubhouse." He pointed
to Retta and formed a solemn expression. "This is one dedicated tomato you have working for you. She put up with a
lot of teasing from me, and I'm impressed."

Retta felt a prickly sensation all over her face and arms
as emotion ran through her. He'd come to the rescue.
She'd never forget this moment.

"Now, really, Dr. McHale . . ." Newt said primly.

"Please, call me Amadeus."

"Uhmmm, yes, Amadeus, I can't really believe this
story of yours, but I do appreciate your gallantry. . ."

"No gallantry, Newt. May I call you Newt? Newt, I
have too much on my schedule as it already stands. I teach,
I'm co-chair of the ethics committee at Rush-Presbyterian,
and of course, as you know, I'm in group practice with two

other cardiologists. I simply don't have the time to take on any duties with your ethics newsletter."

Mac held his hands up in defeat. "But Retta here impressed me so much with her professionalism, and, after I read the material she brought me about National Health, the newsletters, the conference brochures, well . . . I just have to admit that I want to go to market with you on this new newsletter." He paused dramatically. "You need a big cheese for this project, and I'm proud to offer my services."

"Well . . . well . . . super!" Newt bubbled. He was so overwhelmed by Mac's flattery that he nearly bounced in his chair.

Retta gazed at Mac with a humble expression of gratitude. She could be content to spend the rest of her life just sitting there, her body limp with relief, while she looked at him in adoration.

"Retta, I must apologize," Newt said. "If Dr. McHale thinks so much of you—oh, and you know I do also—then I admit that my concerns were unnecessary. While your somewhat unorthodox technique may make the soup a little too spicy, I consider you a good cook."

"I do try," she said quaintly.

"She does try," Mac echoed. As far as he was concerned the discussion had ended. "Great God!" He slapped his thighs and looked at her. "I'm hungry and I want to ask you some questions about this new baby of ours. Let's go to lunch."

"I'd love to . . ." Newt began.

"It was nice meeting you, Newt." Mac stood and shoved his hand out. Newt eyed it a little suspiciously, then took it. "We'll put together a helluva newsletter. A peach." He stepped back, smiled at Retta, then gestured toward the door. "After you."

"I . . . I'll talk to you later, Dr. Winston," she murmured. Newt nodded, his mouth open and unworking. He was outcooked on this one, she thought.

Mac held the door open and she breezed through it,

walking on clouds. Once outside Newt's office she turned around and stopped. She gazed up at Mac with unabashed tears in her eyes.

"Get your purse and I'll wait for you in the lobby," he said gently.

"Why did you do this? It was fantastic, but . . ."

"Shhh. Let's get out of here before Newt comes running after us. He reminds me of sour Jell-O."

Retta covered her mouth to suppress a choking giggle. She nodded, then floated to the stairs that led to the editorial suite.

Five minutes later she was seated in the DeLorean, pulling at the corners of her eyes in a subtle attempt to massage her tears away. Mac swung the silver car out of the parking lot into a windswept Chicago street.

"Are you all right, Henrietta?" he asked. She looked straight ahead, but felt him glancing at her anxiously.

"Certainly. I'm confused, shocked, and overwhelmed. Nothing out of the ordinary."

"I heard that somebody had mentioned the incident to your publisher, and I had to help."

"You didn't have to," she protested gently. "That's why I'm overwhelmed."

"You didn't deserve to be browbeaten on my account."

"I kissed *you*, Mac. It was my fault."

They came to a stoplight at bustling Michigan Avenue, packed with lunchtime traffic. Mac turned toward her, and she looked at him cautiously.

"I asked for it," he said. His voice was low, and his eyes held regret. "I provoked it." He paused. "I wanted it."

She felt a giant tear spread slowly across the bottom lash of one eye. Retta blinked rapidly and looked away.

"But that doesn't change anything you said, does it." There was no question in her words.

"No, it doesn't."

He could almost see the decision flowing into her jaw, squaring it even more. She looked as invincible and as magnificent as a Greek goddess.

"Then I'll be the best friend you ever had." She gazed at him calmly. Her dark hair was styled in its usual backswept way. She didn't use it to hide the strength in her features, and he admired that. She made no attempt to play games. In her beautiful eyes he saw absolute honesty. "I want to be your friend, and I'll behave. You can relax."

A hot and aching tenderness pushed at the boundaries of his chest. This was a woman to cherish. That made it even more difficult to keep his distance. But he would keep his distance, no matter how much it hurt.

"Let's go have a fattening lunch and talk about the newsletter, then," he said with as much enthusiasm as he could pretend. She nodded, then smiled crookedly.

"This is going to be the best damned newsletter the company's ever published," Retta promised. "You'll be proud to be associated with it."

"I already am," he answered, his voice a little hoarse. The light changed and he looked away from her before she could see the emotion in his eyes.

"All right, what does that guy over there do?"

"He . . ." Retta paused, squinting at a plump young man standing at the bus stop. "He raises squirrels."

"Noooo."

"Yes. He looks like a squirrel, Mac. His cheeks are puffy and he's twitchy. I get the feeling he might panic and run into the middle of the street any minute now."

"I say he manages a candy boutique."

"Oh, no. Never."

Mac made a mild sound of disdain at her persistence and immediately got up from the park bench where they'd just shared deli sandwiches and root beer.

"Come on. We'll ask him."

"No. Mac!" He was already walking through the crowded park, sidestepping couples stretched out on the grass. The day was gorgeous, and it seemed as if all of Chicago had come to this Michigan Avenue park to enjoy it. Mac turned around and waved at her to follow.

"This man never met a stranger," she muttered in exasperation. Retta tossed their trash into a nearby can and trotted after him, brushing sandwich crumbs from her navy blue suit.

"Excuse me," she heard Mac say to the squirrel man. Retta stopped beside Mac just as the object of their debate turned benevolent green eyes on them.

"Yes?"

"My friend and I have a bet. I told her I think you run a candy store."

"Why, I do!" The little man beamed at Mac, then nodded to Retta. "I manage the Sweet Things boutique over at Watertower Place."

"That's incredible," Retta said slowly. Mac grinned down at her, obviously pleased with himself.

"See? Don't ever doubt my intuition again, Henrietta." He held out his hand and the candy man shook it. "Thank you, sir, for settling this discussion." They started to walk away.

"Wait, don't I know you, sir?" their new acquaintance called.

"Oh, I don't think so," Mac said quickly.

"Yes, yes, I remember! You've come in several times to buy our gourmet suckers! Thank you for your patronage!"

"Uh, hmmmm, you're welcome." The man's bus arrived. He waved cheerfully and climbed aboard. Retta squinted up at Mac, her lips twisted in an amused, taunting smile. He tucked his chin and looked at her with unrepentant eyes.

"You big cheat," she said. "You enjoy being outrageous, don't you?"

"Is that so bad?" They walked across the park languidly, enjoying the first truly warm spring day. Mac glanced at her as they walked. She was frowning. "You don't think I'm a Peter Pan, do you? Great God."

"A what?"

"A Peter Pan, like your Mr. Put-On-Your-Own-Coat-Baby."

"You mean my ex-boyfriend? Jay?"

"Yep. The guy who never grew up."

"No." She shook her head. "You're not like Jay."

"Then why are you frowning?"

Retta sighed. "Because I'm no fun."

"I've learned to live with it," he said somberly. Shocked, she stopped and looked askance at him before she realized that he was teasing. Retta made a clucking sound with her tongue.

"I'm going to study your technique and try to be more carefree and irresponsible," she told him.

He looked somewhat perturbed. "I'm not irresponsible."

"I don't think you have many worries or many dark moments."

"Oh? I'm not sure I want you to think of me as Mr. Rogers . . ."

A sharp beeping disrupted his words. Mac reached inside his jacket and retrieved a pager. A troubled look had entered his eyes.

"I have to get to a phone," he said quickly.

"I understand." After working with physicians for several years, she knew how important the page could be. "There's one over there."

She waited a few feet away while he called his office. Retta took the moment to study him, memorizing the straight, strong edge of his profile, the thick graying hair that invited a woman's touch, the hint of lean masculine hips under his jacket.

Mac was a man in his prime, very sensually so. Since she'd met him her nights had been hot with fantasies and dreams she couldn't control. Just knowing that this intriguing man felt a similar warmth for her nearly drove her crazy, considering the stubborn distance that he kept between them.

He put the phone down and walked toward her briskly. There was nothing playful in him now, and Retta shivered with awe as she recognized a strength that not only matched, but exceeded her own.

"I have a patient in critical care," he told her without emotion. "He just went into congestive heart failure."

"Don't worry about me. I'll get back to the office on my own."

"I . . ." Something vulnerable and desperate shone for the briefest moment in his eyes. He shook his head, as if rebuking himself. "If you want to come with me . . ."

"Yes."

He exhaled in relief. They hurried across the street to the DeLorean's parking spot. Mac didn't understand his actions, but deep self-examination would have to wait. There was no reason to drag this young woman who hardly knew him into his work. No reason except that the patient who lay dying at Rush-Presbyterian was an old friend, the obstetrician who'd delivered Lucas.

I need her friendship today, Mac admitted silently. I need her.

Retta realized how tense she was when she saw that she'd methodically ripped the prescription blank into quarter-inch bits. It simply wouldn't rip any smaller, and she gathered its tiny pieces into her palm and tossed them into a metal trash can. One piece stuck to her blue skirt, and she examined it distractedly. 'Co', it said. That was all she had left of Vernon C. Cohen, M.D.'s prescription blank. This was Vernon's unoccupied office.

Mac had been gone thirty minutes, leaving her to sit on the wide, low sill of an office window, watching Chicago's midday traffic five stories below Rush-Presbyterian-St. Luke Medical Center. He'd been professional and calm, but underneath she'd sensed his urgency.

Twenty-one years ago the elderly patient who fought for life in the center's cardiac intensive care ward had brought Lucas McHale into the world. Retta considered the fact that she'd only been five years old at the time. She found that an interesting bit of trivia, but no cause for feeling odd about Mac.

The office door clicked open. Retta stood up quickly and kept her expression calm. Mac stepped inside without looking at her, his attention focused on removing the stethoscope that dangled down the front of his sweater. He wearily tucked it into his coat pocket. Retta scanned his face anxiously, her heart twisting in sympathy for him. Defeat had drained away his lighthearted facade, and when his eyes rose to meet hers, they glimmered with sadness.

"He's stabilized," Mac said tonelessly. "But it's just a matter of time." He paused. "Soon, I hope."

She nodded. "He's not in pain?"

Mac shook his head. "No." He crossed to the window and stopped, staring out into a sunny April afternoon that celebrated new life with brilliant blue sky and vibrant green foliage. "This is what we all come to," he muttered. "A meaningless death while everyone else goes about their damned business, unconcerned."

Retta leaned against the window casement and studied the taut angry profile of his jaw. "That's the way it should be," she said gently. "How we die isn't important. How we live is."

"How we die is important." Mac shoved his hands into his slacks pockets and hunched his broad shoulders for a second, fighting the tension there. "I intend to die the way I want to. When I want to. Not like that." He tilted his head in the general direction of the cardiac unit. "Not hooked up to machines, waiting for my body to rebel."

Retta teased him delicately, her voice quiet. "You're going to be one of those cranky old men who leaves the world kicking and cussing and whacking doctors with his cane, I'd bet."

Mac turned an absolutely serious gaze on her, his blue eyes full of resolve. "I'll go quietly, and alone."

Bewilderment and a poignant ache combined to turn her voice into a whisper. "Alone, Mac? What precisely do you mean?"

He faced the window again. "In a nursing home where

I'm certain no one will try to keep my old bag of bones alive for the sake of medical pride. Or my young bag of bones, if I'm run over by a truck tomorrow. I won't die in a hospital with machines doing everything but living for me. I won't be a burden to Lucas." He smiled without warmth. "As some cartoon character used to say, 'Exit quickly, stage left.'"

She frowned. "I understand the part about not lingering when technology has taken over your body, but what is this business about being alone? There's no need for that. You sound as if you want to shut yourself away from the people who care about you."

He nodded. "I do."

Retta felt the sudden sting of air being caught too harshly in her throat. "Why?" she asked, incredulous.

His eyes glittered. "I won't hurt anyone any more than I can help."

She shook her head in utter disbelief and thought of all the warm, loving moments she'd shared with her aunt, even in the final months of Nada's life. "I held my aunt's hand while she died, and I wouldn't trade that memory for anything."

"I held my wife's hand while her doctor disconnected life support, and that's a memory I'd like to kick out of my mind for good. She'd been dead for weeks. It was obscene to put her body through the waiting period."

"Mac." She spoke his name soothingly. Retta understood abruptly that he was confused and still hurt by his wife's death. The fact that he'd cared so deeply for her reinforced Retta's belief that he had a big, loving heart worth pursuing. All this morbid talk of being alone amounted to a passing bitterness. A passing bitterness that she'd overcome.

Retta stepped closer to him and slid a hand around his arm. The muscles felt rigid under her fingers as she squeezed lightly. Easy now, easy, she warned herself.

"Mac, I care about you. You're a very special human being . . . you give so much of yourself to the people around you. Don't shut your friends out when you need them in return." She tilted her head to one side and absorbed the troubled, intense gaze he sent her. Retta was dimly aware of her knees going weak, but she forced herself to offer a wry little smile. "If you're run over by a truck tomorrow, may I please visit what's left of you?"

"You're such a thoughtful friend," he tried to quip.

"I harbor hopes that you'll want me to be more than that one day."

For one incredibly slow moment Mac stared down at her, his chest flooding with a war of frustration and want and self-control. This amazing woman was far wiser than her years, and if he didn't put a stop to her pursuit she'd eventually make him forget all his resolves.

"Haven't you heard anything I've said about myself?" he demanded.

"Yes," she answered, her tone unruffled. "And I'm very patient."

Retta nearly lost her balance as he twisted his body and abruptly took her into his arms. Surrounded by his scent and the powerful pressure of his embrace, she understood for the first time in her life why swooning had been such a popular pastime among women in less liberated times. She felt overwhelmed.

"I could kiss you," he informed her in a low taut voice. "I could take advantage of what you feel for me and coax you into doing almost anything I want. I could probably even play on your affection right now and you'd make love to me on that couch over there." He nodded toward a corner. "I know that."

Retta's face flamed with surprise and emotion. If he was trying to frighten her into retreating, it wouldn't work.

"So do it," she said calmly. "Go ahead."

Exasperation filtered into his blue eyes. "All right."

Retta hadn't really expected him to 'go ahead,' and she cried out in shock when his mouth descended on hers with gentle force. He didn't hurt her, he didn't trap her; he simply poured all his pain into a deep tormented kiss that left no recess of her mouth untouched.

At the same time his hands rose under her navy jacket and curved themselves to her rib cage. Retta cried out again as his palms slid up her cotton blouse and cupped her breasts, squeezing, cajoling, pulling, his touch rough without being painful. The pain was inside her. Retta knew he was teaching her a lesson about his self-control, not offering her pleasure. She jerked her mouth away from his.

"You can let me go now," Retta murmured hoarsely.

"Exactly." Mac took his hands away from her and stepped back, his chest moving harshly. He looked at her in bittersweet rebuke. "I can let you go even after touching you and kissing you because I have a lot more willpower than you think. I wanted to show you that."

"I understand." Aching with defeat and sudden fatigue, she gathered her purse from a large desk near the window.

"You should find someone closer to your own age," he continued doggedly, as if he were trying to convince himself as well as her.

"I understand," she said sincerely. Retta looked up at him with dull eyes. "I chased one man for a lot of years, without results. I won't do it again."

"This conversation won't affect our work together on the ethics newsletter, Retta. I want you to know that."

"Good." She smiled sadly. They'd be quite polite, and the experience would be very cordial. Just like a Soviet-American summit meeting. "I'm glad."

"I'll drive you back to the office."

"No." She held up one hand, and shook her head. "I want to walk."

"No, you don't."

She smiled wryly. "Mac, you've driven me far enough today. Leave me alone." The irony of that last word stung her. "You understand the need to be alone, don't you?"

She stood there hating the sarcasm in her voice, and he stood there hating to be the cause of it.

"I'll see you next week, Henrietta."

"All right . . ." She couldn't continue to be angry with him; she could only hurt because she wanted him so badly.

Retta laughed softly, tears glinting in her eyes. "I'll see you, Amadeus."

She found too much torment in the smile he gave her, and hurried out the door. In the hall she began crying silently. Crying for him, for herself, for both of them being so alive and yet so alone.

CHAPTER SIX

"NOW CONCENTRATE ON the pressure of my fingertips against your forehead," Vanessa urged in low tones that Retta found comical despite her anxiety over their first meeting with Mac. "Let the stress gather there slowly. Slowly. Sloooowly."

Her endearing friend had a high, airy voice, and though she was being perfectly serious Retta thought she sounded like Marilyn Monroe doing a bad imitation of a carnival hypnotist.

"It's gathered already," Retta muttered, her eyes shut tightly, "And it's giving me a headache."

"And you're getting a huge red blotch right between your eyes," Scott interjected from his seat elsewhere in the big conference room. He had a cynical side to him, and could be bluntly honest at times. "You look like someone bonked you with the small end of a baseball bat."

Retta sighed. "Enough," she ordered, and opened her eyes. She leaned back into her plush armchair and blinked several times to readjust her vision to the room's elegant, soft lighting.

Scott sat across from her at the enormous conference table and Vanessa sat by her side, her finger still raised and pointed, as if it were a stress-tracking device she'd attached temporarily to her hand.

"You look more relaxed," she told Retta proudly.

"My forehead muscles are numb from loss of circulation. Of course I look relaxed. I can't even wiggle my eyebrows."

Scott leaned forward with a warning expression in his handsome eyes. "You shouldn't be wiggling your eyebrows, anyway, when Dr. McHale gets here. You said you want us to help you remain completely professional today."

"Leave her alone," Vanessa said, frowning. "She hasn't seen him for a week. If she wants to wiggle her eyebrows at him, she can." Vanessa turned to her and smiled. "From what you've told us, he sounds like a man worth wiggling for."

Retta's love-starved senses nearly overheated from the mental images that came to her. I'm obsessed with Mac, she realized. In the days since their emotional discussion at the hospital her thoughts stubbornly turned to him at every minor provocation. Like now.

She inhaled cool air and focused on watching Scott frown at Vanessa. Suddenly she was sorry she'd poured out her story about Mac to the two of them. They were wonderful friends, but overprotective.

"She barely knows him. I'm trying to help her coexist in dignity with the ignorant bum," Scott said coolly to Vanessa. "If he doesn't recognize a terrific woman the minute he sees one then Retta shouldn't push it—"

"Retta." Becky, the receptionist, spoke over the room's intercom. "Dr. McHale is here for the first planning session."

Retta stood up quickly. She tugged at her tailored white blouse and straightened the bow of a black-and-red pinstriped scarf she'd bought to enliven her black suit. She touched the subtle lipstick on her mouth. I just added some little improvements, she told herself staunchly. To make myself feel more . . . confident about Mac. Yes, that's right.

"Your eyebrows are quivering," Scott quipped.

She shot him a glaring look and pointed to the pastry tray on the gleaming table between them. "Straighten the cream cheese croissants and pour the coffee, you goat," she ordered. "I'll be right back with Mac . . . Dr. McHale. I'll show you two how well I can keep my emotions under control."

"Baaaah," Scott answered. Vanessa laughed gently. Retta swung the room's heavy door open and stepped into the bright afternoon sunlight that filled the hall. Her stomach tight with determination, she looked toward the big lobby that opened off the end of the hall. The sunlight came from floor-to-ceiling windows there.

No. The sunlight came from Mac.

That startled thought ricocheted through her as she caught sight of him, his back to her as he stood in the lobby reading something he held in one hand. Sunbeams burst around the distraction of his tall body and outlined him in a golden halo.

His rich brown hair absorbed the glow and gave it back. His legs were braced slightly apart, allowing a narrow inverted V of sun to emphasize their length. His shoulders were mantled with magic. He was godlike.

Retta brought one hand to her throat and stood rock still, unprepared for such a mesmerizing sight. She'd read that every person carried an image of the perfect mate deep in his or her subconscious. The image rarely coincided with reality, but when it did . . . oh, when it did . . .

She'd cried over him. She'd made resolutions over him. She'd finally adopted an attitude of calm optimism that had erased some of the hurt from last week.

It didn't help now. After thirty seconds she realized that someone was bound to walk out of an office and see her standing there, a stricken spectator. This wasn't just obsession on her part; this was sheer worship. She'd been wrong to think she could be professional and nothing more.

Anger surged through her with such suddenness that she shivered. Stop being a dreamy dolt, she commanded. Are you going to embarrass Mac and yourself? No! She was mad at herself and mad at him, furious with him for doing this to her. She wouldn't let herself stumble up to him in the lobby, exuding worship on his behalf.

Fierce, her throat constricted and her eyes damp, Retta

turned around and shoved the conference room door open again. Scott and Vanessa looked up, surprised to see her come in alone. Retta tapped Vanessa on the shoulder and spoke in a voice that shook.

"Go get Dr. McHale for me, please. I'll see if Hilda and Dr. Winston are ready to come in here."

Defeated and tense, she walked out before the bewilderment in Vanessa's eyes could turn into questions.

Mac heard light footsteps coming across the expensive gray carpet behind him. He took a deep breath that did absolutely nothing to erase his nerves and anticipation.

God, this was going to be hard. He'd spent the past week praising himself for being so noble and logical and responsible, but he still felt the empty ache from watching her walk out of Cohen's office alone. Nothing helped it—not golf, not dinner with friends, not work.

He turned around, intent on being pleasant and very, very formal.

"Retta, how are you . . ."

A small, delicate woman with fluffy black hair and enormous gray eyes looked up at him with a scrutiny he could have sworn was unfriendly.

"Retta, you've changed," Mac joked, and held out his hand. She shook it briefly and smiled without warmth, then introduced herself in a voice that was just as fluffy as her hair and just as cold as her smile.

As Mac followed her back to the conference room he decided that he'd just met a friend of Retta's who didn't approve of him. He suddenly felt like a white-collar Daniel going into a corporate lions' den.

That was confirmed when Scott Woodruff gave him the same curt look and quick handshake that Vanessa Riley had used. Oh, the two of them weren't going to be unpleasant, Mac knew, just icy. He reacted the way he did in all tense professional situations—he turned on the charm.

When Retta stopped outside the conference room door ten minutes later, she heard the three of them laughing. The sound of Mac's deep voice drew goose bumps up her arms. Her jaw tight, her stance showing that she was now ready to battle her emotions, Retta pushed the door open and stepped into the room. Her eyes widened in shock.

He had Scott and Vanessa handcuffed together by one wrist each, and they seemed to be enjoying the experience immensely. They were sitting on opposite edges of the conference table, their hands meeting over the center, and they were grinning like idiots.

Leaning between them, Mac looked up. His calm eyes met her amazed ones. If he was thrilled or distraught to see her again, he gave no indication.

"Hello," he said cheerfully. "I'm just demonstrating my new toy."

With that, he passed his hand over the cuffs and they fell to the table's sleek surface as if released by some invisible power. Scott and Vanessa applauded, and sat down. Retta absorbed Mac's lazy grin with new annoyance. He'd stolen her allies. She was in hell, and he wasn't suffering at all. That was obvious.

"Would you like to try them on?" he joked. "You're the kind of woman who'd enjoy restraint."

"No, thanks." She gave him a stiff smile and sat down. "It's nice to see you again."

She'd rather run bamboo shoots under her fingernails than sit in this room with me, Mac thought in despair. I've certainly short-circuited her affections, just the way I wanted. Why did that ugly black suit have to accent her dark eyes and dramatic coloring so well?

"You look very serious today," he said lightly. "When does the sermon begin?"

Scott chuckled, then had the good grace to look rebuked when Retta glanced at him.

"Have a cup of coffee, Dr. McHale," she ordered in a voice gone deceptively soft. "And let's get started. I know you have a busy schedule, and so do we. Dr. Winston and our executive editor will join us here in just a minute."

Mac absorbed her slight smile and the air of authority she used as a defense. Very subtly, she'd just told him to go handcuff himself to a moving freight train. He nodded.

"I do have some hearts to tinker with later this afternoon," Mac agreed. Scott and Vanessa smiled. Retta nodded back at him with the regal graciousness of a queen being entertained by a mediocre court jester.

We, her royal attitude said politely, are unamused. Under his magnanimous exterior, Mac began to feel frustrated and sad. He flipped open a spiral notepad and almost jerked a slender gold pen from the pocket of his tweed jacket. So this was the way it would be between them.

"All right, let's get to work," he said gruffly.

Retta held the cup of ice against her forehead and hoped that its soothing cold would ease the throbbing pain over her eyes. This was what she now called her standard meeting-with-Mac headache. It blossomed approximately one hour before he arrived, and faded approximately one hour after he departed.

For three weeks she'd suffered. Three weeks, six long meetings, six long headaches. Today would be no different —he cheerful, relaxed, and charming; she authoritative, serious, and half-sick.

A clicking sound announced the activation of her telephone intercom. "Retta," the receptionist said. "Dr. McHale is here."

Little pains, like shards of broken glass, stabbed behind Retta's eyes. She gathered her notes and file folders, then stalked, squinting in discomfort, to Leila's office.

"Do you still have those prescription pain pills you took when you had your root canal?" she asked. "I need one before my head explodes." In a jangle of gaudy jewelry, Leila swung around from her computer terminal.

"If your head explodes you'll look like Hilda. Sure, Tweedy Bird, I've got the pills. But you're not oversensitive to codeine, are you?"

"I'll find out," Retta said grimly, and held out her hand.

She found out halfway through the meeting, when her stomach began to feel like Chicago's Northwest Tollway during rush hour. She'd take her headache back if she could only be rid of this awful nausea.

"Now, the story budget for the first issue has to be like a

good Mexican dinner," Newt was saying somewhere
beyond the sick buzzing in her ears. "Just the right touch of
guacamole, just the right dollop of gooey cheese, the jala-
peño hot but not too hot . . ."

Retta gazed at him in awkward agony. "Excuse me,"
she managed finally, and stood up. "I'll be right back."

Newt stopped cold, and stared at her over his reading
glasses. Hilda tapped her fingernails against the conference
table in nervous surprise. Scott and Vanessa looked up,
puzzled. Retta was dimly aware of Mac's worried eyes
studying her. She smiled at him beatifically, and wobbled
out of the room.

She was halfway down the hall before dizziness overwhelmed her. Feeling cold and clammy, she braced one
hand against the wall and stopped. Wrapped in the ringing
of her ears, she barely heard Mac's footsteps behind her.
His big hands grasped her shoulders gently.

"Going to be sick?" he asked with a physician's nonchalant curiosity. "The Mexican dinner was almost too
much for me, too."

"Yes. And I might fall on my face, first, just as a
warm-up." She was too sick to be professional right now.
"Oh, Amadeus, how did you know? Your trained in-
stincts?"

"Of course." He slid an arm around her and she leaned
against him. "Plus the fact that you zigzagged out of the
room like a disoriented crab. You scared me."

Scared him? He squeezed her shoulder and she knew
that he wasn't being professional, either. He was being her
friend, and she needed that desperately. Retta weakly
tucked her head into the crook of his neck.

"I hope I was a graceful disoriented crab," she muttered
as he led her out the back exit.

The sunshine and crisp spring air had a slightly reviving
effect, and they sat down on the concrete stoop outside the
back door. The traffic jam in her stomach eased a little.

"Head down," he ordered softly, and slid his hand into
her hair. Retta yielded to his steady, easy pressure, and put
her head on her knees, her face buried in her hands.

"There," he quipped. "Now you can upchuck on your own shoes, instead of mine."

She smiled a little. "I'm not so nauseated, anymore. Now I'm just embarrassed."

He kept his hand against the nape of her neck, and his strong fingers rubbed the taut skin. "I could bounce pennies off the muscles here. Are you having a migraine?"

"No. I'm having a reaction to the codeine painkiller I bummed off a co-worker for my ordinary tension headache."

He was silent for a moment, and when he spoke again he sounded grim. "You should know better, medical editor."

Mac slowly put both hands on her neck and began a serious massage. Her skin felt like satin over steel cable. It cried out for the sensitive attention of his lips. Mac closed his eyes and allowed his mind to drift pleasantly.

Retta groaned. Whether she was sick or not, this was too much. His touch was a torch that brought heat to every part of her body. Considering how clammy her skin felt, steam might rise off her.

"Please stop."

"Did I hurt you?" he asked.

"Yes." She raised her head and looked at him sadly. "You did."

Mac studied the agonized intensity and the dampness in her eyes, and knew that she wasn't referring to his massage. She looked frail and helpless for just a second, and his hands drew around to her face, cupping it tenderly.

"You'll be all right," he said without conviction.

"Not if you keep touching me. Please stop, Mac."

He hesitated, wanting desperately to say to hell with good sense and capture her in his arms. Instead, he trailed his fingertips off her cheeks and grasped her right hand out of her lap. Mac pressed two fingers over the pulse point in her wrist.

"You're icy cold," he noted, his voice low and gruff.

"It's my nature." Her joke was grim.

"Hardly." He paused, silently counting. "Your pulse is

up. Don't take any more painkillers that aren't prescribed for you. You ought to go home for the rest of the day. I'll take you."

"You will not. I have work to do. Let's go back to the meeting."

"I've had all I can stand today. The meeting's over," he said tersely.

Retta was shocked at the anger in his normally sedate voice. She took in the harshness in his eyes and frowned. "I thought you were having a ball at these meetings. Everyone adores you."

His blue eyes burned into her. "You don't."

She swallowed hard. "You asked me not to adore you, if I recall."

His fingers against her wrist were warm channels for the emotion that flowed between them. "I know," Mac whispered. "But that doesn't make it easy to live with."

"But you seem so damned cheerful all the time!"

"Here." He wrapped her fingers around his own wrist and positioned her fingertips over the pulse. "Check this out." For a moment Retta was only aware of the feel of thick, masculine bone, ot skin, and tight sinews. Then she gauged the racing, hard rhythm of his blood. She released his wrist and stared at him in mute sympathy.

"I'm torn up, too," he told her, his eyes shadowed. "I hurt. I leave these meetings with a fist in my stomach that won't let me eat at night."

She wavered for just a second, surprise running through her. Then she made a low, soothing sound and slid her arms around his waist. They hugged tightly, her face turned away from his so there'd be no unstoppable temptation to kiss him.

"This is only a professional hug," she noted. She locked her hands together to prevent their wandering. His hands dug into her slender back as if resisting the urge to stroke her.

"I'm only hugging you because you're sick, and hugging is therapeutic," he joked weakly. "And because we're friends." And because I'm absolutely crazy about you, he added silently.

"I've been behaving, haven't I, Amadeus? And I'll continue to behave. I'm trying very hard to be as noble as you are."

She felt his warm breath against the nape of her neck. His hands tightened, started to slide down her back, then halted with rigid restraint.

"You're my inspiration. You've behaved to the point of being a glacier," he said sadly.

"Mac," she groaned. "I'm sorry, I know I've been un-friendly. It was just because..." Her voice filled with wistful exasperation. "I'm afraid that if I let myself relax around you I'll do or say something I shouldn't. I do want to be friends. I just don't know how to be."

"Of course you do. Treat me like you treat Scott." She sat back a little and looked at him. Mac thought hard for a moment. "Flirt with me."

"I don't flirt," she said with dignity.

He gave her a patronizing look. "You do, too."

"I've never fluttered my eyelashes or simpered in my entire life, McHale."

"You touch Scott's arm when you talk to him. You lean toward him when he talks to you. I'd appreciate a little of the same."

Retta tilted her head and studied Mac's somber expres-sion for a moment. "Are you jealous?" she asked in an incredulous tone. Mac McHale was too together, too calm, too easy natured to be jealous. She hoped fervently that he was jealous as hell.

"Envious," he corrected, arching one light brown brow. "I want to be your friend. I can't stand the way you've treated me for the past three weeks. You smile at me with-out meaning it. You avoid looking into my eyes. You sit as far away from me as you can get. I might deserve it, but I don't like it."

"Oh, Mac, I didn't intend to hurt you. I was just trying to be honorable."

"Be honorable, but don't treat me like pond scum."

He drew his hands off her and stood up. Retta accepted the grasp he offered and he helped her to her feet. She touched his jacket sleeve with dramatic slowness.

"I'm practicing harmless flirting with you," she said whimsically.

"You'll get the hang of it," he told her.

They shared a soft, bittersweet laugh and started back inside. Never, she thought sadly.

But over the next two weeks she admitted that things had relaxed between them, that they could, on the surface at least, just be friends. The newsletter preparations progressed by leaps. Mac was invaluable, brilliant. Newt was thrilled. Hilda, tyrannical at worst and moody at best, was almost jovial.

Retta called Mac one afternoon to invite him to a celebration dinner Newt had suddenly planned for the whole advisory board.

"It'll be at Maxine's," she said proudly. "Truffles, *foie gras,* fine wines—the works."

"The bribes are getting more expensive."

Retta laughed. She seemed to be laughing a lot these days, and feeling more optimistic about Mac all the time.

"All the advisory board members will be there," she told him. "And Scott, Vanessa, Hilda, Dr. Winston . . ."

"And you?" Mac asked.

She preened. Oh yes, friendship was blossoming right along. Hope springs eternal in a medical editor's heart, Retta thought happily.

"And me. I'm going to sit beside you and lean toward you when you speak to me. And touch your arm."

He laughed softly, and she sighed with pleasure. They talked on and on, about golf, about Lucas's hilarious fascination with professional wrestling, about imported beers and Bill Cosby and the *New York Times* book reviews.

It wasn't the first long converstion they'd had via the chaperoning conduit of the telephone. Oftentimes she called him or he called her with some trivial question related to the newsletter. They'd settle the question immediately and then plunge into rambling, relaxed discussions that would only end when work interrupted.

The phone calls were getting so routine that Retta began to plan her afternoons around them. Now she had something else to plan—her appearance for the dinner. Oh, boy, was Mac McHale in trouble. She hummed with anticipation.

It was black. It was velvet. It cost two hundred of Retta's hard-earned dollars and when it slid sensuously over her cool skin she knew it was worth every one. The dress wasn't inappropriate for a Thursday-night business dinner, but on the other hand, it made her usual plain suits look like burlap sacks.

Standing in the middle of her bedroom, Retta crooked her arms behind her and slid the zipper closed. Now the dress felt indecently snug, but when she gazed at her reflection inside the antiqued frame of a long mirror she saw just an intriguing hint of upthrust breasts and curvy hips. The V neck dipped to the edge of her modest cleavage, and the long, simple sleeves made her arms look as graceful as a dancer's.

"Honey," the salesclerk had said, "every woman needs a little black dress for special occasions."

"For provoking Mac to wild extremes," Retta added now, and smiled. She felt the full force of the power she'd been accumulating during the past two weeks, the power of certainty. Nothing he could do or say would shake her confidence now. He wanted her as badly as she wanted him and all she needed to win him was patience and dignity. And a little black dress.

She slid her legs into opaque black hose sprinkled with black dots. She'd wanted with wicked raciness to buy tall, black, stiletto heels, but that would have been too outrageous.

Besides, she was going to draw Mac into dancing with her, and she didn't want to risk teetering over, heels to the winds. So she tucked sedate black pumps onto her feet.

Retta fastened Nada's long strand of antique pearls around her neck and placed her mother's small diamond wedding ring on her right hand. This was her best jewelry, special jewelry because it flooded her with warm, good memories. She wanted Mac to see it. She looked forward to telling him about it.

Smiling whimsically as she assessed her uncharacteristic excitement, smiling at the world and at the prospect of pretending to be Mac's dinner date tonight, Retta hummed as she left her apartment building and climbed into her car.

"Wow!" Standing in the elegant, Art Nouveau bar at Maxine's, Scott grasped her hands and stepped back from the little black dress for a good look. Retta knew her eyes were gleaming as she enjoyed the appreciative study from this skilled ladies' man. And she knew the glow inside her was puny compared to what she'd feel when Mac's eyes roamed over her this way.

"And your hair!" Vanessa exclaimed. "It's so curly and loose!"

"That's the way my head feels," Retta whispered. "This is so different for me!"

"Yep," Scott agreed drolly. "And I like the change. Being in love is just what you needed."

"Love!" Retta protested, her mouth hurting from the wide grin it tried to contain. "Love!" Sweet sensations filtered through her like honey filling an empty honeycomb. "No!"

She couldn't put that name to the way she felt. It was too soon, and she was too practical to jump to conclusions about her emotions, and she had too much work to do on Mac's overly principled, misguided heart.

"She's grinning like a Cheshire cat," Scott told Vanessa. "Either she's in love or she's just had her teeth cleaned."

"Mingle," Hilda hissed, as she walked past them.

The three of them were momentarily ignoring Newt's instructions to blend, to socialize, to stir the soup. Most of the ethics newsletter's advisory board had arrived and were milling around the sleek white bar, sipping cocktails compliments of Newt.

"We'll show Hilda 'mingle,'" Retta promised cheerfully. She spread her hands in a grandiose directive to Scott and Vanessa. "Sic 'em, editorial hounds."

"Woof," Vanessa added.

Laughing, the three of them headed in different directions. Retta chatted with other members of the ten-person advisory board while she kept one eye on the bar's graceful, arching entranceway. Where was Mac? He was late, which wasn't normal. She bubbled with anticipation.

A minute later Mac stopped in the archway. His hands sunk in the pockets of his black slacks, his shoulders a little slumped, he searched the crowded bar with guarded, troubled eyes.

He saw Retta, her back to him and her profile turned just a little to reveal her dark, upswept lashes and classically straight nose. He blinked swiftly, then looked again while his heart stalled in his chest.

Mac's eyes roamed over the clinging dress, her tousled hair, the creamy pearls scooping a white oval against the firm thrust of her velvet-covored breasts. He nearly groaned out loud from the emotional and physical response that shuddered through him.

She'd dressed in a way that was totally contrary to her staid, adorable image to please him, he knew without doubt. Sorrow became a terrible ache inside him, but the pain made a harsh smile come to his mouth. He deserved to suffer for what he was about to do to her.

Retta quivered with a delightful psychic sensation. Immediately she looked up, and as she'd expected, she found Mac's tall, proud body framed in the doorway. He presented a perfect picture of masculinity in a gray jacket and black trousers, a dark tie dividing the creamy white of his shirt.

Casual, controlled, fantastic, she thought in quick succession. Distinguished by the gray wings in his hair, he was sophisticated and very, very virile. Every female in the bar was looking at him.

His blue gaze centered on her with disarming attention, and she quivered again. We're telepathic, she teased him silently as she wound her way between tables, smiling.

Kindred souls. Reincarnated lovers about to join in another new life together...

A tall, elegant, blond woman stepped into the perfect picture and slid her hand around his elbow.

CHAPTER SEVEN

RETTA HESITATED, SHOCKED and puzzled. Take your hand off his arm, she thought blankly. That arm belongs to me.

A subconscious pride as strong as gravity forced her feet to keep moving forward as she killed everything but polite curiosity in her expression. Vague impressions came to her about the very misguided woman still clasping Mac's arm.

Porcelain pretty. Walking proof that women over forty were tremendously sexy. Expensive red silk dress with shoulder pads. Slender hips, long legs. Heavy gold jewelry wrapped around a delicate throat and frail wrists. Disaster. Grief.

"Well, Amadeus, I'd almost made up my mind that you'd decided to go polka tonight instead of coming to dinner," Retta said glibly. Hidden emotions jerked at the muscles in her throat.

He assessed her graceful recovery from the sheer shock that had crossed her face and looked down at her with intense respect.

"No, we're just running a little late," he murmured. "I'd like you to meet Isabella Edwards. Isabella, this is Retta Stanton, the assistant executive editor at National Health."

"Hello," Retta said in a welcoming tone. Mac's "we're just running a little late" stabbed into her. He'd brought a date. Retta was incredulous.

She extended a hand gone ice cold; Isabella extended hers and shook with no inkling that she was staring into the hazel eyes of a bewildered enemy.

Isabella smiled gently, and Retta thought of a fragile jonquil about to sway in a breeze. The woman was so incredibly attractive, so blond, so casually elegant, so tall—so much like a picture Retta had seen of Judith McHale.

Retta nearly swayed as fear raked her spine. She couldn't compete with this. She granted herself one desperately nosy question cloaked in chitchat.

"Isabella, where has Mac been hiding you?"

Her eyes—blue eyes, like Mac's—crinkled merrily. "Oh, we're on a blind date. We just met today."

"Ah. I see." It didn't help, Retta thought. Isabella still had Mac's arm, and why had Mac done this cruel, humiliating thing anyway? She looked up at him with what she hoped was a neutral gaze.

Mac quietly withstood the intense pain and betrayal that radiated from her dark eyes. "You remember me mentioning my friend Greg Conway, the Delta executive?" he said softly. "His wife is a self-appointed matchmaker who brings unsuspecting women to my lair."

Isabella laughed pleasantly, but vacantly. There isn't a mean bone in this creature's svelte body, Retta thought suddenly.

"Do you work for Delta?" Retta asked her.

"Oh, no. My late husband did, however. I travel quite a bit now."

She said that as if traveling were her full-time job, which meant she was probably wealthy. She was perfect, Retta thought in anguish. Independent, adorable, probably passive and undemanding. Perfect for a man who wanted an older woman and no burdensome worries about relationships.

"Folks, this has been just a lovely happy hour," Newt suddenly announced. "But our table's ready and I'd like everyone to follow me into the dining room for a lovely dinner."

"Lovely," Mac tried to joke.

For the briefest of seconds Retta pinned him with a wistful gaze that told him not to attempt humor when she was dying inside. Then it disappeared behind her old formality.

"Well, excuse me," she said in a strange, high voice. "It was nice talking with you both. I have to go."

"You can't go too far," Mac said urgently. "I mean . . . we're all sitting at the same table."

"Well." She paused; when she spoke again her voice was low. "It's a very long table. I might not have a chance to talk to you again."

"Oh, I love your ring!" Isabella exclaimed abruptly. She stretched delicate, inquisitive fingers out as Retta lifted her hand for inspection. "An heirloom?"

"Yes. My mother's wedding ring."

"The diamond's of such quality! It sparkles much better than mine." She held the pea-sized diamond on her right forefinger next to the minuscule stone on Retta's hand.

Retta studied her sharply, expecting to see something catty and rude in her eyes. But there was nothing, just sincere congratulations.

"It's beautiful," Mac interjected.

"Thank you," Retta murmured. Her eyes burned with frustration. "Really, excuse me."

"You promised me truffles and *foie gras* tonight," Mac persisted. He couldn't let her walk away. He'd done the smart thing, the right thing, by bringing a dinner date, but he could barely keep from hating himself at the moment. He forced a teasing smile. "You'd better deliver on your promises."

The corners of Retta's mouth curved up. Her gaze didn't rebuke him for bringing this stranger here to act as a human wall between them. Instead it presented a clear window through which he saw her deep sense of defeat.

"I keep my promises," she told him, smiling bravely. "You know that." With a final nod to Isabella, she walked out of the bar.

I know that, Mac agreed grimly. *Now I'll never have to worry about it again.*

Retta walked lifelessly through Maxine's white-on-white, coldly intimate dining room. Given a few minutes away from Mac and his date, she knew she could regain her composure. The drowning sensation behind her eyes would ebb away. Her hands would stop quivering as if she suffered from palsy.

At a long table in one dimly lit corner, Newt was directing everyone to their chairs. The tendril of a hanging fern kept reaching for his smooth cheeks, and he kept pawing it away with a petulant gesture.

"Retta, I'd like you to sit here at my end of the table," he said crossly, and popped the fern away again. Retta reached up and stroked its delicate greenery out of Newt's way. Poor fern, she thought irrationally. Poor . . . poor fern.

Her mouth trembled and she sat down abruptly, jerking her napkin into her lap and unfolding it with meticulous attention to detail.

"And Mac, you sit here, with this charming lady next to me . . ."

Retta lifted disbelieving eyes to watch Isabella Edwards pour an intrigued smile onto Newt as he helped her into the chair directly across the table. No, Retta groaned inwardly. Not across from me. And Mac . . .

He slowly lowered himself into the chair next to Isabella, his eyes meeting Retta's in abject apology. After a moment she smiled at him wearily, as if to say "All right, it's unpleasant for you, too. I understand."

Newt went down the table with prissy elegance, telling grown men and women with doctorates and master's degrees where they had to sit. Retta found Isabella's blue eyes on her, full of excitement. Isabella leaned across the table.

"Dr. Winston is the epitome of style, I see. Mac described him to me."

"Why . . . yes," Retta answered slowly. *Newt's the epitome of something,* she added grimly. *I hope we find a cure for it.*

"Have you worked for him long?"

"Four years." It seemed ages. *The pyramids were new*

when I came to work for Newt, Retta thought. *Or maybe I've just grown ancient in the past five minutes.*

"Is he always so in command?"

"Oh, yes." He's the General Patton of publishing. Retta frowned at the sarcastic tone of her silent responses. Isabella was truly nice. Truly sweet. Almost childlike. She probably slept in baby-doll pajamas. Would Mac find out?

Newt returned and sat down at the head of the table. He smiled at Isabella and she smiled back. Retta raised her brows and studied the undeniable exchange of energy between them.

Mac shifted in his chair and Retta couldn't keep her eyes from going to him. He propped one elbow on the table and his chin on his hand. She knew he was trying desperately to be nonchalant.

"What are you shooting these days?" he asked.

She wanted to answer, "Your date," but instead she murmured, "I broke a hundred yesterday on the Greenbriar municipal course."

His eyes flickered with admiration. "Remind me never to bet against you."

"You never collected your prize from that time we played together," she said fiendishly. "The lollipops."

Isabella tore her gaze away from Newt to smile at him uncertainly. "You like lollipops?"

"He's addicted to them," Retta added. She smiled in a jaunty way that said she knew all his intimate habits, and they were so droll.

She forced herself to meet Mac's gaze. Retta lifted her chin with a very subtle show of daring. She saw bittersweet amusement spread across Mac's face as his eyes continued to hold hers. I can survive this awful thing you've done, her attitude told him.

Come on, doll, his responded. I'm proud of you. Do it. You're great. He looked at Isabella and nodded, his smile pleasant.

"I love lollipops," he confirmed.

Isabella smiled, then turned her attention back to Newt. "You men," she bubbled girlishly. "You're just as whimsical as we are. In life's orchard, the persimmons are just as sweet as the peaches, but the persimmons won't admit it."

Retta's mouth opened to an "Oh" of recognition at the food analogy, so much like Newt's. She watched Newt lean forward, a strange, awestruck gleam in his eyes.

"I find that analogy," he said in a gruff voice, "profound."

Isabella blushed like a snow cone absorbing strawberry syrup. She bit her lower lip and looked at Newt from under her eyelashes.

"Thank you," she murmured. "I find that much of the human condition can be expressed in poetic terms concerning fruit."

Newt looked at her without blinking. "Tell me more," he said in hoarse tones.

Retta casually trailed her eyes over to Mac's. His repressed need to laugh at Newt and Isabella in the midst of this tense, sad night had colored his tan pink and straightened his lips into a line of defense. His strong jaw shifted, settled, then shifted again as he fought back the same astonished chortles that Retta felt in her tight throat.

They sat there, lost in each other's eyes, caught between laughing and crying, while Isabella and Newt chattered like fruit flies on holiday.

"Retta! Retta, wait."

Scott's voice made her stop at the entrance to Maxine's bar. Inside the dusky bar a few advisory board members lingered for after-dinner drinks. When she'd left, Mac and Isabella were seated close together at a small table. Newt had been seated close together with them.

Retta looked up at Scott and saw the concern in his eyes. Any other woman would melt into her panty hose over the look in those green eyes, Retta noted silently. She only felt numb. He pulled her to one side so that a giant ficus tree provided some privacy.

"I thought you'd left," he said gently.

"Euphemistically speaking, I went to powder my nose," Retta answered.

He brushed a thumb across the slightly swollen skin under her dark lashes. "You should go back and euphemistically powder your eyes," he joked.

A tremor went through her, and her shoulders slumped. "It's obvious, then? That I've been washing my face from the inside out?"

"It's not too bad. You're still the best-looking woman here."

"You want a raise. Okay, you got it."

They laughed, sharing a comfortable affection that made it easy for him to put his arms around her. Retta clasped her arms tightly around his lean waist and burrowed into the friendly warmth of his shoulder.

"Go ahead," Scott whispered. "Pretend I'm Mac."

"Thank you," she whispered back.

Mac felt the strangely empty pressure of Isabella's hand on his arm as they walked toward the bar's exit, and he wished for the hundredth time that he could think of a diplomatic way to say, "Stay with Newt. I don't mind."

Because he couldn't, and because she apparently couldn't think of a diplomatic way to say that she wanted to stay with Newt, they were leaving together. He knew that they'd say good night at her condominium's door and then she'd come floating back here to discuss kumquats and bananas.

And where the hell had Retta disappeared to? She'd obviously used the powder-room pretense to slip away and go home. Tired, depressed, and tense, Mac led the fluttery Isabella out of the bar.

He automatically swept his gaze around the restaurant's lobby. The sight of Retta snuggled deep into Scott Woodruff's arms, her eyes closed and her expression content, twisted his stomach.

"Ummm, good night, Retta," Isabella called hesitantly.

Retta winced. Where Isabella went, Mac was likely to be also. Quickly she told herself that Mac was too wise to be angry over this innocent scene. And he had no damned right to be jealous. She opened her eyes and looked directly into Mac's piercing gaze.

"Yes, good night, Henrietta," he added. He's jealous, Retta knew immediately. The undercurrent of frustration had nearly choked his beautiful voice. She felt grimly victorious.

Scott gracefully let her go and she stepped back without hurrying. You have no right, McHale, she thought again. She let her gaze bite into him with reproach even though she curved her mouth into a pleasant smile.

"Good night, Mac. It was nice to meet you, Isabella."

Mac wavered for a split second. Then his mellow nature went up in a bonfire of emotion. He turned to Isabella.

"Would you excuse me for just one minute? I have some business to discuss with Retta. I'll be right back."

"Oh, of course," she said happily, and headed into the bar again.

Mac grabbed Retta's hand and glared at Scott. "Excuse us," he told Scott crisply. "Why don't you go home?"

Scott was no one's lackey. Even though Retta knew that he liked Mac, he wouldn't be bossed.

"I'll wait for you," Scott said to her.

"Do," she replied, her expression grim.

Retta let Mac tug her all the way to a quiet alcove before she snapped her hand out of his. They faced each other, breathing heavily in a fierce, matched rhythm.

"I expected better from you than a thoughtless tactic like that," he rasped. "Aren't we friends?"

"So we are," she rasped back. "And so are Scott and I. A hug between two friends isn't a tactic, McHale. It's a hug. And don't parade your date in front of me and then act possessive."

His eyes were blue fires.

"You wouldn't do something foolish like use Scott for a little desperate comfort, I hope," he whispered roughly.

Retta felt embarrassment and increased anger burn holes in her complexion. "Thanks for giving me the idea." Her voice was so anguished it was barely audible. "I would never ask you if you intend to take the fruit queen home with you. Never." Her eyes were full of tears that she prayed wouldn't fall. "It's none of my business. You don't want it to be any of my business."

He seemed on the verge of exploding over the inner battle with his principles. Finally, he got his voice to come out in a calm semblance of its normal self.

"I just don't want you to do something you'll regret, simply because you're angry or hurt with me. I'm asking you, as your friend, not to turn to someone just for comfort."

Retta raised clenched fists and shook them at him. Her voice was a hoarse, fervent whisper. "I've been alone for more than two years, Mac. I need to be held. I need to have a man make love to me. I never realized how much I needed it until you came along." Tears slid over her lashes. "I never realized how little warmth I have in my life until I saw how much warmth you have to give."

She shoved her hands against the lapels of his gray jacket as she looked up at him in torment. "But you don't want to give it, and I won't beg. I won't." She released the smooth material twisted under her fingers, pressed her hands to her forehead, and stepped back. A soft moan escaped from her throat. "Just don't ask me not to look for someone who can keep me from going crazy over you."

"Not Scott," he said desperately.

"Scott's my best friend. I'd never complicate that. He was hugging me because I was upset, Mac."

"Fine. Then you're too upset to drive. I'll give you a ride back to your apartment."

She looked up at him sardonically. "And lock me in, m'lord? To protect me from my own base desire? Fie! Whenst the apartment janitor doth wander past my door, I'll trick him in and have my way with him!"

"Don't joke," he ordered. "I care about you so much . . ."

"Then help me be what you want!" she begged. "If you just want to be my friend, don't act like a jealous lover!"

All the spirit drained out of him. She was right. He was going insane and taking her along with him. He reached forward and cupped her face in his big hands. For a second he massaged her tears into the pads of his fingers, absorbing her grief through his skin.

"I have to go back to Isabella," he said hoarsely.

"I'm going home." Retta fought the urge to turn her face to the side and kiss his caressing palm in an abject show of devotion. "Alone."

"Thank you. And rest assured that I have no intention of getting cozy with the fruit queen."

Her eyes pinned him with all the honesty in her soul. "Some night I won't go home alone, Mac, and if you happen to be around when that happens, don't repeat this scene. Don't ever question my personal life again, all right? You owe me that privacy."

His hands tightened around her face, and for a moment she thought he was going to pull her toward him. She'd go, she'd leap, she'd assure him that no man could take his place. But he released her and stepped back, his eyes full of anguish.

"I owe you that," he said raggedly. "You're right." He drew his hands from her face and walked away, taking all the warmth in the world with him.

Shush, shush, shush. The scrub brush made hearty cleaning sounds on Retta's white windowsills. Her teeth gritted, she pressed both hands harder on the brush and shoved it back and forth in a froth of pine-scented cleanser that spattered the stretch band of her plain, moon-faced wrist watch.

The time display caught her eye. Twelve-thirty A.M. on a weeknight. A perfect time to scrub the sills, she thought sardonically.

The little black dress lay nearby in a heap on the scrolling flower print of Nada's handsome old sofa, where she'd flung it two hours ago. Its accoutrements—the shoes, hose, and jewelry—rested on top in a scattered pile.

Retta was beginning to feel too warm in the ankle-length granny gown she wore. She jerked up the gown's tail and tucked its bright print material into her white panties, leaving her short but lithe legs to cool. What was the good of being five feet seven with short legs? she asked apropos of nothing.

"Who cares about long legs?" she said tautly. "Or glamorous black dresses." Tears stung her eyes and she fought them back. "Who cares about men? Who wants to be bothered?" She scrubbed harder. Who cares, who cares, she chanted silently, in rhythm with the brush. Shush, the brush said.

When someone knocked at her door the sound startled Retta so much that she fumbled the brush and it clattered to her varnished wooden floor., With eyes full of puzzlement and dismay, Retta stared across her cozy living room at the door's white panels. Who in the world waited on the other side of those panels at this time of night?

The knock came again, "Just a minute, please," she called. Retta distractedly pulled her gown tail out of her panties and hurried into her bedroom. She came back wearing a robe and carrying a small automatic pistol. A gun, she and Nada had decided long ago, was a practical accessory for urban life.

The door had no peephole. Retta leaned against the cool wood, her gun pointed toward the ceiling. She stepped back mentally and assessed the picture she presented. Despite her fatigue and depression, it almost made her smile. Dirty Harry in a granny gown.

"Who are you?" she asked the visitor in curt tones.

"Mac." There was no mistaking that endearing voice.

Her gun hand dropped limply to her side. Retta unlocked the door, her heart pounding with anger. He had come to make certain she was alone. Damn him. She pulled the door open and scaled him with a brief look. Her voice shook with outrage.

"I'll never forgive you for coming here, Mac."

His eyes were full of torment and he was frowning. His gaze roamed over her and stopped at the pistol. Grim humor touched his mouth.

"Retta, you can make me dance, but I refuse to polka anymore."

She reached over to a squat little lamp table beside the

door and left the gun inside its shallow drawer. Then she faced him again, her back squared and her eyes cold.

"I'm alone. Good night."

She started to shut the door, but he took a step forward to make that impossible. Retta felt her fingers clutching the door's edge with painful force. He continued to look at her with a frown that drew his brown eyebrows into a flat line.

"I didn't come to check up on you."

Retta wavered as surprise hit her. Speechless, she stared at him for a moment. He still wore the handsome gray jacket and black slacks from hours earlier, and they were so unwrinkled that she wondered if he'd sat down at all since she last saw him. His graying brown hair was rumpled as if he'd been running his fingers through it haphazardly. The lean, intelligent face she knew so well was haggard.

He was the picture of a man who'd been tearing himself apart over decisions, she thought suddenly. Her breath caught in her throat and made her hoarse.

"What did you come here for, then?"

Retta took a step back. He advanced. One of them shut the door—she didn't notice who. Mac looked down at her with somber, determined eyes.

"To ask you to run away with me tonight."

He took another step toward her and she retreated again, the shock of his simple words driving her toward the safety of Nada's homey 1940s living room furniture.

For the first time since she'd known him, Retta thought of Mac in primitive terms of male aggression. Suddenly he seemed very intense, very starved for her. He had a dark, worried look in his eyes, as if he wondered what he might do.

Retta sat down weakly on the old couch, next to her rumpled black dress. Mac sat down on the other side of the dress. He reached out and scooped up the pearls and her mother's ring.

"These are beautiful," he said gruffly. "They suited you tonight. Sexy and old-fashioned at the same time. You nearly drove me out of my mind. I knew you were hurt when Isabella compared that huge rock of hers to your mother's diamond."

"Why are you here . . . really?" His kind words made her feel worse. Retta clasped her hands in the center of her lap and kept her back schoolmarm straight. She simply didn't believe he'd come here to run away with her. A mixture of anger and sadness made hot pools of sensation inside her.

Mac dropped the jewelry back on her dress. His blue eyes sought her hazel ones and she saw apology for his erratic behavior, but also determination.

"I can't let you go looking to some stranger for sex," he said sternly. "You're no more nonchalant about bedroom things than I am."

"You *are* here to check up on me, then," she emphasized. Retta gave him a weary, rebuking smile. She'd just tell him the truth, and he could take his gallant protection the hell away. "Don't worry, Amadeus. I'm an old maid at heart. A conscientious objector in the sexual revolution. Just because I act like a sex-starved beastie around you doesn't mean I'm going to wrestle the janitor next time I see him. I was only joking about that. You can go home now."

"Stop it." The tension in his voice wiped the wry smile off her face. His eyes hard, Mac took one of her hands in a firm grip. "Look straight at me. Don't look away," he commanded.

Retta complied, her chin up proudly. "Now listen to me, Henrietta. I can't go on like this, wanting you all the time and fighting it. I've spent the last two hours talking to my conscience about you. I promised myself after Judith died in such a damned horrible way that I'd stay away from involvements. I promised myself that I'd grow old gracefully and alone. And I promised myself I wouldn't chase young women."

"You're a mite young to be growing old gracefully, Amadeus. And you haven't been chasing me, I've been chasing you, remember? Your conscience should be clear. Please go home."

She tried to pull her hands away, but his grip tightened painfully. Retta stared at his strong fingers in shock. As if sensing her alarm, he loosened his hold slightly. Mac sighed.

"I already feel senile. I'm not making much sense." He cleared his throat. "My conscience and my noble decisions held up pretty well until I met you and fell in love."

Now Retta's fingers dug into his and she looked at him wretchedly. "Don't tell me that," she begged. "If you want me to keep one shred of dignity where you're concerned, don't tell me that you love me."

"Give up your dignity. I'll give up mine, too. It's all a bunch of nonsense anyway—I act noble when really all I can think about is having you. Your intelligence. Your sweet little formal ways. Your body."

Those last words made her feel as if everything inside her was being rearranged into an aching, receptive jumble of sensation and emotion that only his touch could soothe.

"Well," she said, stunned. "Well." Oh, God . . . he really was offering her everything.

"Now I've scared you," he said morosely. "Love is a lot more than you bargained for."

Retta began to shake. He was so dear and so befuddled. "Mac," she whispered, leaning toward him like a distraught conspirator, "I fell in love with you the day we met."

His eyes widened. A disbelieving smile began to ease across his mouth.

"Oh, I know I'm being whimsical," she added quickly. "I suppose I couldn't really fall in love with a stranger. I mean, logically speaking . . ."

"Retta, Mr. Spock is less logical than you. Be illogical," Mac interjected. He began to laugh, and looked so relieved that sympathy surged through her. His old exuberance rose to the surface and brought a glow to his eyes. Suddenly he stood up and stepped in front of her, then bent in one fluid motion and took her face between his hands.

Retta's whole field of sensation narrowed down to the feel of his long fingers against her cheeks, the smell of his cologne that she'd long ago memorized, the hypnotic pull of his eyes. Her lips parted and her eyelids felt heavy with desire. This was almost as intimate as making love. She put her hands over his.

"I don't know if it's right for us to be together," he told her hoarsely. "but you came into my life like an unexpected gift, and I can't bear to give you back."

He paused, searching her eyes. An uncharacteristic wildness rippled through him, and he knew he had to kiss her very soon. "Run away with me and see if you like being coddled and adored by an older man."

"Your age has nothing to do with the kind of coddling and adoring I want," she teased weakly. Incredulous happiness seemed about to burst her chest. "Are you serious, Mac?"

"Yes."

Her knees went weak. Dreams could come true. She spoke breathlessly. "Perhaps . . . you could give me a demonstration of adoration, Amadeus, so I can judge."

"Certainly." He forced himself not to hurry. His breath ragged, Mac leaned forward and very slowly tilted her face up. Retta closed her eyes and touched her tongue to her lips in anticipation. She nearly moaned when Mac slid his thumb across her damp mouth, spreading the moisture, preparing her.

"Here it comes," Mac whispered, just before he touched his mouth to hers. Lightly, his lips tugging with delicious roughness, he brushed back and forth—deliberately tormenting her, it seemed. She sighed in delight. After several seconds, she pressed forward and slid her tongue into his teasing mouth.

Mac groaned at the sensation and grew still, enjoying her intense exploration, then returning it when he couldn't wait any longer. He had the urge to tilt her head back and press rough, hungry kisses all over her slender neck, but restraint—this intimacy was so new, so fragile—was an unspoken agreement between them. Her fingers squeezed rhythmically around his wrists; her tongue curled around his with erotic skill.

With this woman there would be times, he knew, when desire would tear away all inhibitions. He gave in a little and slid his mouth down her neck, tasting her skin, inhaling the scent of her smooth, dark hair as it brushed his face. Quivering, Retta put her arms around him and reveled in her new permission to stroke his shoulders.

"So are you going to run away with me?" he asked in a throaty murmur, his mouth against her ear. "Even though I make no sense at all and my principles are in shambles?"

Mac sat back from her on his heels and languidly slid his hands down the front of her robe. Retta stopped breathing as his palms rested briefly on her breasts, then traveled to her waist and waited, their grip tight and provocative even through her clothes.

She nodded, smiling crookedly and stroking the beautiful silver hair at his temples. Her eyes followed the motions of her fingertips.

"When do you want to leave, Mac?"

"Tonight. Right now. As soon as you can pack a few clothes. It's Friday morning. We'll take a long weekend."

She looked at him then, her eyes wide as if he'd proposed a strange experiment. "How far are we going to run? Isn't this . . . extravagant?"

His eyes amused and loving, Mac shook his head at her practical words. "This is very special, Henrietta. I don't want work or friends or anything else to intrude on our first few days together as lovers."

That did it. She was a goner. She'd never wanted this sweet, sensitive man more than at this moment. "Together," she repeated in awe. "Oh, Mac, I love you so much."

"I love you, too," he whispered.

She hugged him fiercely, and he moved up to the couch beside her and pulled her into his lap. Her bare feet rested against the old, florid upholstery of the sofa's armrest.

Mac fingered the hem of her soft granny gown for an amused moment, then slid it up a few inches and rested one hand on the shin of her leg. The small new intimacy made him quiver inside. He rubbed the pads of his fingers against the smooth skin just below her knee.

"Oh," she murmured, half moaning, and closed her eyes.

"Retta?" he asked anxiously. "What is it?"

"Your hand on me."

"Is it cold?"

"No. It's wonderful."

When she opened her eyes he was staring at her in happy amazement. He smiled devilishly, then spoke in a low, emotional voice.

"What would happen if I moved my hand higher?"

"More than you can imagine in your wildest dreams, Amadeus."

"My God." Both of them were shivering as they kissed again. He tugged his mouth away and said fervently, "Henrietta, we have to get this affair started, but this couch looks too old to . . . it might not survive. Let's get out of here before we forget that. Where do you want to go?"

She shook her head. "I can't, Mac. And you can't. What about your patients?"

"My two partners owe me more favors than they can ever repay. They'll take over for a few days." He stroked her hair. "God, this is the color of chocolate. And when it's wild like this . . ."

"But I have a meeting with Hilda tomorrow . . ."

"You're getting very sick," Mac intoned in a hypnotist's lulling voice. "Very sick. You can't go to work tomorrow. You need a day's vacation." He slid his hand inside her robe, and she gasped as it flattened just above her left breast. "Be still now, and let me make a diagnosis."

Retta closed her eyes and thought raggedly, If you let your hand move farther down you'll find an acute case of aroused nipple.

"Ah, yes," he said, and nodded somberly. "That's a sad, starved heart. It's been hurt a lot lately by some idiot. I wonder who."

"I heal quickly," she replied.

"I prescribe a combination of fine food, expensive

hotel, coddling, adoration, and bed rest mixed with exercise."

"Whew! Wherever will I find such a potent remedy?"

Mac trailed his hand up to her neck and stroked the pulse point at its base. "Wherever you want to go with me. My treat."

She kissed him with such tenderness that he felt as if their bodies were already joined. "You can't pay. It seems improper for you to spend a lot of money on me. We'll go dutch."

Mac chuckled. "Lighten up, Miss Henrietta Manners. Don't you harbor the least bit of greed for all my dough?"

"No!"

He nodded, his expression drolly serious. "I'll have my work cut out, then, teaching you to accept presents." He made himself look sad. "Won't you grant an old man one simple wish?"

He was so absurd that she burst out laughing. "All right, all right, this one time." Her eyes gleaming, she bit her lip and tried to think of intimate vacation spots. There'd never been much money for such things in her life. "I know!" she exclaimed. "We could drive down to Peoria."

The affectionate exasperation in his eyes rebuked her. "Think big," he instructed.

"Springfield?"

Mac sighed. "There are other states beside Illinois, you know."

"But we only have three days . . ."

"Man and woman get in great silver bird," he deadpanned. "Fly into starry night. Morning come, bird land in faraway place."

"Oh," she said weakly. "That kind of running away."

His teasing faded. "Honey," he murmured, "where have you always wanted to go? Just name it."

"Honey," she echoed with a smile. "I love you."

Grinning, he gave her a boisterous kiss. "Dammit, honey, where?"

"Disney World, in Florida," she said sheepishly. "I've always wanted to meet Mickey Mouse."

After a startled moment, Mac threw back his head and began to chuckle. The chuckle grew into deep, hearty laughter. Tears rolled out of the corners of his eyes. Retta smiled, then grinned, then leaned her head against his shoulder and laughed along with him, stroking the soft material of his shirt as she did.

"I'm trying to forget that you're sixteen years younger than me," he finally managed. "But you're not helping."

"Look, McHale, I'm not a kid. After Mickey, I want to see the science and history exhibits . . ."

"Sshhh. I'm only joking." He slid his hand behind her head and rubbed soothingly, apologizing. "I've always wanted to meet old Mickey myself."

"Mac." Her voice dropped to a sultry whisper. She pressed her lips against his ear and nibbled the lobe. Under her, nudging her hips, she felt the intriguing ridge of an aroused male body.

Mac grew still, then allowed his hips to arch gently against her. She exhaled in a rush of pleasure. His hands stroked her lower back as he spoke in a hoarse voice.

"What, beautiful?"

"If we never find time to go to Disney World . . . if we spend a lot of time in the hotel room . . . will you be disappointed?"

He shivered and held her tightly. "Hardly," he murmured. "There are some entertainments that Mickey Mouse can't even begin to compete with."

CHAPTER EIGHT

Shuh-click.

Every cell in Retta's body reacted nervously to that muffled sound as the door to the Orlando hotel room locked behind the departing porter. Somewhere a few miles outside that door lay Disney World. Just a few feet away on this side of the door stood Mac, his attention focused on something in the sleek leather wallet he'd pulled out when he gave the porter a tip, seconds earlier.

Retta stayed absolutely still, her plain, boxy purse cupped in one hand in front of the simple skirt and blouse she wore. Her eyes roamed over the incredible room. No, this wasn't just a room, she corrected silently. It was a suite, with a cozy, chandeliered dining room to the left. It was an invitation to indulge in luxurious pleasure.

The furnishings were contemporary and very plush. Everything was done in soft maple colors and earth tones. A sumptuous king-sized bed sat a little to her left. Short brass lamps on the bedstands promised to provide elegant, sensual lighting.

In one corner of the room a fully stocked bar built of some rich, gleaming wood waited. A Jacuzzi sat in another corner, the floor around it and its sides covered in russet earthenware tiles. A cabinet on the wall nearby was stocked with towels and massage oils and only God knew what else.

Probably a miniature masseur who'd pop out any minute and ask if they wanted a morning rubdown, she thought blankly.

Her gaze kept moving. There was an inviting couch and coffee table in front of a window that covered one whole wall, and even though they'd checked into the hotel at six A.M., there were fresh flowers on the table. The porter had opened the window's heavy curtains, and the sheers underneath were colored pink by the faint dawn light.

Far to her right, an enormous bathroom beckoned her to be adventuresome and try its bidet. She'd glanced in that sophisticated bathroom on her first quick inspection of the suite, and been overwhelmed. It had a television set. Indulge, this place whispered.

But Retta didn't know how to indulge. She didn't know how to deal with luxury now any better than she had the day at Mac's country club. And this was infinitely worse, because this time Mac would realize how out of place she really was.

So she continued to stand absolutely still, looking back and forth between the only two comforting sights in the room—her familiar brown suitcase and Mac.

He slid the wallet inside his gray jacket—the jacket he'd been wearing since Newt's dinner the night before—and slowly raised his eyes to hers. The somber, tender look he offered her faded into a concerned frown.

"Henrietta? Are you all right?" he asked softly.

"Oh, sure." She clutched her purse a little tighter and blinked rapidly. Mac looked at her with puzzlement. She was the kind of sturdy soul who never allowed fear to show, but now her eyes were large and dark with it.

No, please, God, she's not having doubts about us, is she? he prayed silently. Mac walked toward her gingerly, as if she were a skittish horse he wanted to calm.

"We'll take it slow," he murmured. "Relax."

"I'm . . . I'm sorry . . ." she began plaintively.

"Sshhh." He watched as her mouth stayed open for a moment, then closed. A frustrated, sad expression touched her face. Mac's stomach churned as he considered what she might have said next. I'm sorry, Mac, maybe we shouldn't be doing this? Maybe we should just continue to be friends? God, that would rip him apart.

He put his arms around her very carefully and was alarmed to find that her back felt as rigid as a board and she was quivering. Mac took a moment to gather every shred of kindness and warmth he possessed.

She looked up at him with a gaze of pure misery and continued to hold her rigid little purse right where it was, like a blockade to keep him away, he thought anxiously.

"I know you're exhausted," Mac murmured. "We should have napped on the plane instead of talking all night."

Retta's reverence for his voice reached new heights. She had never heard it sound quite so soothing before. It poured over her taut muscles like hot butter.

"Are you cold?" He studied the goose bumps on her arms beneath the short-sleeved white blouse she wore. "You shouldn't have taken your sweater off." Because he was worried and didn't know what else to do, he kept talking. "This place is fantastic, isn't it? I knew we could trust the recommendation of any cab driver who had a heart tattooed on his forehead." He kissed her forehead. "Maybe we should turn on the Jacuzzi and—"

"I'm scared, Mac," she said in a small voice.

Mac stared down at her in anguish for a moment, until solid determination took over. All right. She was admitting her doubts, and he could deal with that. He could fight for her.

"Retta," he murmured in a sympathetic voice. "We'll just take it easy, like I said before. We'll just enjoy being friends, being together, this weekend. I could even get a separate room—"

"Mac!" Her voice was full of shock. "It's not *you* I'm afraid of. It's this place."

Stunned, he couldn't talk for a moment. "You don't have any doubts about us?" he asked finally, feeling dazed.

"Oh, honey, of course not. I adore you." She tossed her purse onto the bed, then slipped her arms around his waist.

Retta wrapped herself to him as snugly as she could, the whole length of her torso melting to him, and nuzzled her face into the crook of his neck. She quivered harder.

"Retta, Retta," he cajoled softly, while he ran his hands over her back and arms in a rhythmic, relaxing motion. He knew now how much what she felt and thought affected him, because he wanted to quiver along with her. "What's wrong with this hotel? We can go somewhere else."

"No, that would be cowardly. I'll adjust," she promised. She was so whimsically brave that he smiled into her hair.

"Would you have felt like this in Peoria or Springfield?"

"No. I wouldn't have to contend with Jacuzzis and bidets and potty TV's there. This luxury, Mac . . . I'm afraid of it." She pulled her head back and looked up at him with despair. "It makes me realize how unsophisticated, how plain I am. I don't want to embarrass you."

He wanted to chuckle, but she was so upset that he couldn't. "Honey, last night when you walked over to meet me in the bar at Maxine's, did you notice anything odd about the men in the room?"

"No."

"Well, they all have sore necks today from craning their heads to watch you. You're not unsophisticated or plain."

"I'm plain in here," she said, and pointed to her head.

"You're a classy lady who never had the time or the money to learn how to enjoy life, and I'm going to rescue you with all sorts of gifts and attention."

"I'm no good at accepting gifts when I can't reciprocate."

He gave her a teasing look. "Retta, what's the good of me being a wealthy older man if I can't indulge my sweet young thing?"

She couldn't help smiling. "I'm not a sweet young thing."

"I know, but humor me, Retta. I have my fantasies."

They looked at each other silently, balanced on the edge of nerves and exhaustion and giddiness. Mac nodded toward the bed.

"I prescribe sleep for these worries of yours," he said

solemnly. "And I mean sleep—we keep on a decent amount of clothes to fight the temptation to play show and tell, and we snuggle up and sleep for about three hours. Then you call your office and I'll call mine again just to make sure my half-awake partner absorbed what I told him on the phone last night."

Her old no-nonsense attitude returned, and she nodded firmly. "Of course. That's the logical thing to do."

He slid a finger under her chin and stroked its strong outline while his gaze roamed over her lovingly. "Don't get used to being too logical, Henrietta. It's not going to be a very logical weekend."

The color had begun to return to her face. Her eyes glinted with warmth. "I'm practical enough to know when to throw logic out the window."

They laughed gently, then kissed with a sweet, close-mouthed tenderness. Mac felt stubborn desire in his loins, and he willed himself to ignore it. Rest first, romance later, when she felt more comfortable.

On some silent signal they released each other. Retta exhaled in resignation and looked around the suite again. As long as Mac understood and sympathized with her awkwardness, she'd be all right. Maybe this place wasn't so bad. It was no Peoria, though.

She fumbled with her skirt while Mac walked to the curtains and closed them. The room seemed very dark and intimate, suddenly. Her hands shivered as the skirt slid to the floor. Retta could feel Mac's eyes on her and a thrill of pleasure zipped across her navel. She went to the suite's huge closet and hung the skirt up, then kicked off the flat brown shoes she wore.

Out of the corner of her eye she watched Mac remove his shoes and socks, his jacket, then his tie, then his shirt, then his black trousers. She almost gave up all pretense, wanting to stare wantonly once his tall, trim body was covered in nothing but a T-shirt and white boxers.

The man had incredibly long legs, covered in dark hair. That same dark hair, dusted with gray, curled over the V neck of his shirt. He put his leather tote on the massive dresser across from the bed and unzipped it.

"Do you want to hang your suit up, Mac?" she asked breathlessly.

"Nah. It's hopelessly wrinkled. I'll get it pressed sometime today." He paused. "Quit ogling me," he instructed drolly, without looking up. "You're going to get some rest. We're going to sleep. And that's that."

"Egomaniac. I wasn't ogling you."

Smiling, she removed her blouse and hung it in the suite's huge closet.

"Good Lord . . . you should have warned me, Henrietta!"

Mac's startled comment made her jump. She faced him, feeling worried. "What is it, Mac?"

His eyes trailed down and then back up her body, and she knew the answer. Retta tucked her chin and studied her dark blue silk slip with its lacy, diaphanous bosom. Under the slip, hidden from his eyes, she wore an equally lacy bra and panties. Wait, she thought wickedly, until he sees those.

"My secret whimsy," she admitted. "Fancy lingerie."

As nonchalantly as she could, considering that she felt his eyes follow every move she made, Retta went to one side of the bed and pulled back its thick coverlet and top sheet. She sat down on the edge of the mattress and fiddled distractedly with an alarm clock on the bedstand.

The thick, comfortable mattress felt wonderful, she thought. Here it was, the place where their bodies would meet, where she'd revel in Mac's weight pressing on top of her, where . . .

"Here." Mac's voice, very close to her, made her look up quickly. He cocked a brow and looked very determined as he held out one of his white undershirts. "The doctor prescribed a remedy for your nerves and he's going to make sure you get it." He cleared his throat. "Sleep, that is. Put this on."

She smiled fiendishly. "Instead of my underthings and panty hose?"

His blue eyes lit with exasperated amusement. "Over your underthings, you sassy dame."

Chuckling, Retta took the soft cotton shirt and slid it over her torso. "It smells like you, Mac," she said softly. "Thanks. I feel a lot more relaxed."

"You're welcome."

Their eyes met and held as she slid her feet onto the bed. She moved toward the center of the mattress and slowly stretched out, pulling the covers up to her waist as she did. Her senses registered the intensity of every second.

"The patient is waiting, Doctor," she murmured.

"Why do I think you're going to be difficult to treat?" Mac asked in a low voice. The look in his eyes as he slid into bed beside her was so warm she wondered what kept the sheets from igniting where they touched her skin.

He propped himself on one elbow and leaned over her, smiling. His hand came forward and his fingers curled into the hair above her left ear. Something velvety soft stroked her cheek, crossed her parted lips, and caressed the end of her nose. The scent was unmistakable.

"A rosebud!" she said in awe. "Where . . . how did you do that? Where did you have it hidden?"

He held the tiny, red flower up for her perusal. "Magician's secret," he said somberly. "It's an enchanted rose. When I touch you with it you'll fall asleep and dream sexy dreams about me. Close your eyes."

She had never felt less like sleeping in her life, but she did as he asked. Under the dark shield of her eyelids, her other senses became acutely alive. Mac nestled one of his long legs next to hers and the curly hair prickled her delightfully, even through her hose.

She heard the somewhat uneven rhythm of his breathing, and measured the motion of his chest as it swelled against her arm, against the side of her breast.

"Sleeeep," he intoned in his most seductive voice. He touched the silky soft rosebud of her forehead, then trailed it back and forth across her eyes. It pulled delicately at her eyelashes.

"Dreeeam," he said even more languidly. Retta felt every muscle in her body relax. This was magic. This man was magic. But now she was keenly awake and very aroused.

The rose outlined her lips with infinite attention to detail. She sensed Mac studying her mouth, and knew from the increased rhythm of his chest that he found it nearly too tempting. The thought of his desire brought a soft whimper to her lips before she could stop it.

"Sleep," Mac whispered hoarsely, the strain evident in his voice.

He trailed the rose over her chin and down her neck, first down the center, then back up one side, then across and down the other, then up to tickle one earlobe, then down to the fluttering pulse point between her collarbones.

Go on, go on, she begged silently, as his fingers paused over the base of her neck. Slowly the tips stroked the sensitive skin at her pulse. His next words sounded almost groggy with emotion.

"This is not the pulse of a sleepy person," Mac informed her.

"No." She put a world of meaning into that answer. "But I am . . . relaxed. Don't . . . stop."

For a breathless moment he didn't answer. The rose tickled her throat again. "I can't stop," he nearly groaned. "I'm afraid the prescribed treatment has failed."

A tremor ran through her, and she bit her lip from the pleasure of anticipation. "Good."

He dipped his head close to her ear. "Keep your eyes closed, beautiful." She nodded weakly.

His hands grasped hers and pressed them into the pillow above her head. Retta sighed happily as he drew the soft T-shirt off her body. His leg slid between her knees and she squeezed it. Then the rose began to draw lines of fire on the tingling skin above her breasts.

"Oh, Amadeus," she whispered, her eyes still closed. "You're burning me up."

"I'll take more of these clothes off you, then," he murmured devilishly. "To . . . make you feel better."

"Oh, yes."

He brought her arms down by her sides and slipped his fingers under the straps that held her flimsy slip and bra up. He drew the straps toward her elbows, every movement as slow as honey slipping down a warm spoon.

His voice throaty, he ordered, "Tell me what my touch feels like."

"Rough silk," she said breathlessly. His fingertips slid under each of her arms and hooked into the lacy bodice and bra. Retta gasped as he pulled the material tight across her supersensitive breasts, then eased it down, scrubbing her nipples roughly, deliciously. Cool air soothed her feverish skin as she lay half-bare under his gaze.

"Plain," Mac whispered in gruff rebuke. "You think you're plain. My God, Retta." His voice dropped. "My God, you're incredible."

In response she made a soft moaning sound. He quickly touched the rose to her again. He spent long minutes tantalizing her nipples with it, caressing the undersides of her breasts with languid strokes, teasing her stomach. Then his lips followed the rose.

He began to describe in loving detail everything he saw. Perspiration coated her skin and she shifted under his touch. Hours seemed to pass as he finished undressing her, and by the time the last inch of wispy clothing trailed off her feet she was moving in ecstasy.

He stretched out beside her again and let one hand stroke her, reaching down her thigh and sliding up the inside, lingering at the top. The rosebud dropped apart, leaving dewy red petals on her stomach and in the pliant hair under his fingers.

Those fingers went on tormenting, exploring, cajoling her while his voice offered loving encouragement.

"That's it, Retta, my beautiful Retta . . ."

When a magnificent ache began to gather inside her she opened her eyes and found him looking directly at her, as if he'd been waiting. His skin was flushed dark with desire and his eyes had gone so blue they seemed like summer sky. He was the picture, the essence of her pleasure and her love.

"Please, Amadeus," she whispered plaintively.

He understood her simple words and pulled his hand away from her writhing body. His eyes closed, he lay back and let her remove his shirt with the same sensual patience he'd shown her.

When he made a rough sound of delight she leaned over him and dropped a damp kiss on his parted lips. "I wish I had a rose for you," she murmured against the firm, ruddy contours. "I'll have to make do without one."

He smiled, then arched his head back as her mouth brushed down his body. Her lips traced the indentation of a taut muscle in his stomach. "Nothing old about this," she assured him. The flat, brown disks of his nipples turned darker under her wanton tongue. "Nothing old about that," she teased.

Her hands slid around his lean sides and carefully pushed the boxer shorts down his thighs. There was a pause of discovery.

"Oh, Amadeus," she said in absolute wonder. "You're in your prime."

When she cradled him in her hands, his breath shattered the intimate silence of their room. A long moan followed. "Retta," he gasped. "I didn't know there was this much pleasure in the world."

"Just wait, my handsome man, just wait," she promised in husky tones. "There's more." She made him arch again as she ran her hands down his thighs. His boxer shorts were removed in a slow ceremony of caresses, and when he lay as naked as she was, she knelt beside his feet and simply worshiped him with a silent examination.

He got up and knelt facing her, his knees on either side of hers, his eyes showing the starved, primitive look she remembered from earlier, at her apartment. They were both breathing harshly as he grasped her arms.

"Don't let me be too . . . lusty," he asked. "I've never felt this uncontrolled before and God knows I don't want to do anything rough."

Puzzled, Retta looked at him without answering. Then an even greater tenderness welled up inside her. "Mac." She stroked his cheek. "You're the most unselfish man I've ever met. But when you're with me, be selfish. Take pleasure from me. I have so much pleasure to give you. Be as lusty as you want."

She raked his mouth with a desperate kiss.

"I love you," he said with a hoarse groan, and pulled her into his arms.

They fell back on the bed in a jumble of intertwined limbs and exploring hands, all patience gone. Retta arched and twisted against him as his tongue delved deep into her mouth and his hands squeezed her breasts.

He pressed her onto her back and her legs surrounded him with welcome. He threw his head back and cried out, "Easy, easy," warning himself.

"No," she begged. "I'm yours. I'm ready."

His head slumped forward and he met her eyes with a fiercely loving gaze that she returned. She rose to meet him as he plunged into her. He cupped her head in his hands and covered her mouth and neck in deliciously savage kisses punctuated by his moans.

"Mac, oh Mac," she said in her last coherent effort before words had no meaning. The tumult inside her began where the center of her body met his and grew until she had to clasp his heaving sides for balance.

Somewhere in the midst of their turbulent passion they kept a gentle retreat, and when she made a high-pitched, keening sound of ultimate release he touched worshipful fingertips to her lips and called her name softly.

Retta felt like a phoenix—burned to ashes and reborn —as she dimly heard her voice fade away to soft murmurs. She drew his head to her shoulder and his harsh breath filled her ear. His body pumped hard against her, and she shivered because her pleasure was still exquisite.

"Now you," she urged. "Now you, Amadeus McHale. My love, my lover."

The hoarse sound he made shattered hotly against her neck and grew into a shout of happiness as he convulsed once, then again, and finally shuddered to a stop with his hands knotted in her hair.

"You've broken me up and put me back together," he whispered several seconds later, as she kissed the moisture off his neck. "I'm brand new." Retta stroked his shoulders with quick, light caresses and smiled against his damp skin.

"Then we're the same age," she told him.

He raised his head and they shared a solemn look of agreement.

"Oh, no, no . . . get away, Mac!"

"Wear it, pleeease, just for me?"

"You made me polka with Goofy. You made me harmonize with a group of singing, mechanical bears. That's enough for one day!"

"Pleeease," he wheedled in his deep, luscious voice. "It's very sexy."

Retta sighed. How could she refuse that voice, those eyes, that freshly showered body clothed only in white shorts? They sat cross-legged on the hotel bed, facing each other. She reached into the jumble of souvenirs spread out around them and picked up the familiar black cap with round, black ears on top.

"All right, just for a minute," she said wryly, and put it on her head. She couldn't believe the giddy fun he inspired. She'd never acted this way before. Retta began to sing. "M-I-C . . . K-E-Y . . ."

"It's Annette Funicello!"

Giggles overwhelmed her. She doffed the Mouseketeer hat and rolled over on her side, her knees drawn up and her hands covering her mouth. Laughing, Mac crawled over to her and kissed her boisterously. He tickled her bare thighs with his fingertips.

"Stop!" she protested halfheartedly.

"You're lying here all clean and dewy in nothing but a Mickey Mouse T-shirt and you expect me to behave?" he demanded. Smiling, he rolled over on his back and put his hands behind his head.

Suddenly her mouth was against his ear, nibbling. "I'll teach you a lesson," she whispered devilishly. "Provoke me, will you?"

The mood changed from playful to intense over the space of a second. Desire stayed so close to the surface that since the first time, yesterday, it had blossomed repeatedly, induced by the tiniest of gestures, the simplest of words. He started to put his arms around her, but she pulled back.

"No," she said, smiling at him. "I want to do something different."

"Don't put the mouse hat back on," he teased hoarsely. "It isn't that sexy."

"No mouse hat," she agreed. Mac gasped as she burrowed her mouth into the thick hair above his navel and began teasing his skin with her tongue.

"What . . . Retta . . . what are you doing?"

"Well," she said huskily, "I thought it was time I showed *you* a magic trick . . ." She raised her eyes to look into his as her fingers rippled over his taut muscles. "It's called conjuring unbearable desire out of thin air. What do you think?" she murmured, dropping her head and brushing her hot, searching lips across his flat belly.

"I think you're a magician," he moaned softly, as his body began to move.

She stood patiently in the elegant hallway, holding her Mouseketeer hat and her suitcase while he unlocked the door to his condominium. He turned a searching, slightly worried gaze on her before he opened the door.

"No residual anxiety?" he asked. "You aren't going to panic at the sight of more luxury, are you?"

She smiled benignly. "You don't have a television in your bathroom, do you?"

"God, no," he answered, chuckling. She nodded.

"Then I'll manage."

He slid his free arm around her and pushed the door open with the leather tote bag. Retta absorbed quick impressions. A foyer. Low, serene lighting over gray slate tile and smoky walls. A huge but cozy living room, very American traditional—radiant mahogany, brass fixtures.

She noted fat couches and chairs covered in dark blue leather, dark amber walls behind photos encased in simple cherry frames—all of Lucas, none of Mac or Judith.

No artwork; a few richly colored tapestries; long, packed bookcases; endearing masculine clutter; russet carpet so thick it made her step gingerly. Two sets of double doors led to a wide garden room that looked out over Lake Michigan, more than thirty stories below them.

"You have style, Amadeus," she whispered. "And warmth. I want to wrap this place around me and hibernate."

"Good," he whispered back. His hand caressed her arm. "I'll show you the hibernation room."

She inhaled the subtle presence of his cologne even before they entered the master bedroom. More dark colors and rich woods, Retta thought languidly, while Mac put their luggage on a big dresser. A king-sized bed for his long legs. A brass ceiling fan over the bed. More bookcases. When did the man find time to read everything Elmore Leonard and Ellery Queen ever wrote? she wondered, smiling. They walked toward the bathroom.

"Now, be calm," Mac said somberly, as he flicked a switch that poured soft light into the area.

She gasped dramatically. "A sunken tub and a sauna! Oh, be still, my plain little heart."

"Your heart can relax," he told her, smiling tenderly. "I'm going to give it expert care."

"Free exams?"

"Yep. Very personal."

"I think I feel a palpitation, Mac."

His mouth barely suppressing a smile, he picked her up. "Then I'd better put you in bed and listen to that adorable little ticker of yours. Test it, see how it responds to excitement."

She put her arms around his neck and hummed into his shoulder. A few minutes later, when her clothes lay in a jumble and his thick, smooth bedspread caressed her bare back, she whispered coyly, "Mac? How can you listen to my heart that way?"

"My lips feel subtle vibrations in your valves," he murmured. "It's a new technique."

Retta let the familiar, simmering heat fill her body. This was a luxury she'd have no trouble learning to enjoy.

CHAPTER NINE

IT WAS FRIDAY night and they were working late, as usual. No one else was around.

"Scott?"

Retta watched him run a hand through his deep forest of light brown hair. His forearms, exposed by his upturned shirt sleeves, were thickly muscled from lifting weights. Bicycle racing kept his long legs lean inside his tan sacks.

He was gorgeous and he had lots of experience with women. If any man had the answers she needed, he did. He looked up from a paste-up table identical to the one at which she sat. The table's bright fluorescent light backlit the production board for his newsletter.

"Yes?"

"Do you ever want to get married?"

One corner of his mouth crooked up in a sardonic smile. "How long has it been since McHale swept you off to Mickey Mouse land? A few weeks? Are you looking for a new man already?"

"No, you teasing bum. Don't flatter yourself. I'm in need of your advice, but I have to gauge your qualifications, first."

"Hmmm. No, I don't ever intend to get married."

"For goodness' sake. Why not?"

"Because I'll always be a cynical, woman-chasing lecher."

"No, you're just a cynical woman chaser. Not a lecher. I think you're sort of lost and lonely."

"Well thanks, Retta. Please, don't beat around the bush. Tell me exactly what you think of me." She studied him with a wistful frown as he winked at her. Under all his calm competence was a wounded soul.

"My father was married four times, Retta. I'm not a good man to ask about marriage. Besides, until I get out of school with my master's degree I'm too broke to be a good marriage prospect."

"Well, you're the only man I know well enough to pester about the subject." She took a deep breath. "If you were in favor of marriage, and if you had fallen deeply in love with someone, how long would you wait before you proposed to her?"

"About a hundred years," he quipped. "And then I'd insist on a prenuptial agreement and a long engagement." When he saw the anxious look in her eyes his sardonic attitude ebbed away. "Sweetness, it's a little early for you to worry about McHale. Isn't everything just ecstasy between you two?"

She nodded, and knew her eyes must be gleaming. "I don't know how I could live without him. That kind of ecstasy."

"Whoa!" Scott shook his head in grim rebuke. "Don't ever say that about anyone."

"It's true. And I believe it's mutual."

"He was married for a long time, Retta. He might want to sample the wild life now. He might not ever want to remarry."

"He's not that way. Before he met me, he'd hardly dated at all."

"That worries me even more. It's not natural."

She gave him an exasperated look. "All men aren't as unscrupulously hormone-driven as you, Woodruff. Don't call Mac 'unnatural.'"

"Okay, okay." He shook his head in self-rebuke. "I apologize. But Retta, don't bring up the subject of marriage with him. Give it time. I suspect the man's got a long way to go."

She lowered her eyes and fiddled distractedly with a sheet of waxed newsprint. "You're right. I will. Nobody is more patient than I am."

Retta tried to force her worries away. They were together almost every night, weren't they? He treated her like the focal point of his life, didn't he? And in today's world, nobody much cared if people got married or not. She was just too damned old-fashioned.

"Retta Stanton McHale," she murmured under her breath. She'd like to see that name on two or three birth certificates. And it'd look very stately on her tombstone one day, and in genealogy books. Everyone would know that she'd loved Mac until the day she died, and even afterwards. That's why she wanted to bear his name.

"What's that you said?" Scott asked vaguely. He'd returned to his work.

"Oh, nothing," she answered, and bent over her own work again. She was going to marry Amadeus McHale, that's all.

There was something awfully distracting about a man's frontside cozying up to a woman's backside, Retta thought with mild annoyance. Especially when they were standing on the driving range of Mac's prestigious country club, surrounded by a dozen other golfers, the golf pro, and his assistants.

She was trying to perfect her golf swing and Mac was supposed to be helping her. His arms lay warmly on top of her arms in the hot June sun. His palms moved with suspicious intent over the backs of her hands. And he was certainly enjoying the game's terminology.

"The shaft," he said into her ear, "should extend up toward the inside of your thigh. Put your left hand . . . oh yes, right there, ummm . . . on the shaft's target side. Now, with a firm grip, you're ready to stroke . . . ."

"I'm not ready for anything," she answered in amused disgust, "except to thump you with this driver."

He laughed, and his breath tickled her ear. He stepped back. "Go ahead, see if you can do it alone."

"I'll show you," she retorted. She bit her lip in concentration, adjusted her stance and her grip, and swung hard. The instant her ancient wooden driver connected with the golf ball she felt the wood splinter.

"Oh, no," she said in despair. Retta tenderly grasped both ends of the prized old club and stared at its mangled middle wretchedly. "Oh, no."

She felt Mac's anxious grip on her shoulders. "Did you hurt your hands?" he asked. She turned around and held the club out as if he might be able to heal it somehow.

"No, my hands are fine. But look at my mother's club, Mac."

He tried to joke. "We all have to go sometime."

Immediately, he knew he'd said the wrong thing. Tears of rebuke filled her eyes. His hands slid down her arms in a soothing gesture. "Honey, I apologize."

She nodded, and her expression turned wistful. "When I was little I must have watched my mother swing this club a thousand times." Retta paused, struggling not to cry. "I can still see her . . . she had hair the color of mine, but long . . . and she let it stay loose. It would . . . float . . . in the air . . ." Retta gestured weakly with one hand. "And I can see her smiling with this happy look in her eyes . . ."

"Don't, honey . . ." he ordered gently.

" . . . and that's the only really vivid memory of her I've been able to keep. This . . . club was like . . . it was something she and I could still share."

"Come here," he murmured, and drew her to him for a sympathetic embrace. Tears crept down her face and she stood there with her forehead against his shoulder, feeling like a forlorn child who'd just broken a very special doll.

Mac glanced up and caught the disapproving looks of several fellow golfers, mostly svelte older women in designer outfits. They reminded him of sleek housecats with dangerously mature claws. They had no idea why he was hugging Retta, but it was obvious that they were either jealous or offended by the display of affection.

He recognized one of them as having nearly cornered him at last year's club Christmas party. And she was married, for God's sake. Another was Jean Conway, the notorious matchmaker whose last project had been Isabella. In a way, Jean's matchmaking had worked out. Isabella and Newt were living together in culinary happiness.

"Hey, McHale, get a hotel room!"

Startled, then angry, Mac turned his gaze toward the sound of that crude comment and found Allen Dewberry stalking toward them from the clubhouse with a grin on his puckish face. Retta stiffened in his arms, then pulled back and began wiping her face briskly.

"Oh, Lord, I'm sorry."

"Sshhh."

"Introduce me, Mac! I want to meet the little girl who teased you out of your self-imposed exile from women."

Mac counted to ten. "Allen, proctology suits your personality," he said in a flat voice. "Retta, this is Allen Dewberry. Allen, this is my friend Retta Stanton."

"And Mac said you two were just business acquaintances," Allen teased and chortled as he grasped her hand. She gave him a bewildered, annoyed frown, which he missed as he squinted up at Mac. "Decided you liked grapes did you, you old sonofagun?"

Allen grinned back at Retta, totally oblivious to good taste, Mac thought desperately. He'd apparently indulged in his Saturday martinis already.

"When I asked about you a while back, Mac said he preferred vintage wine, not grapes. But if I've told him once, I've told him a hundred times, a young woman will do more for the soul than a vitamin shot. Got one myself —a young woman that is, not a vitamin shot. She spends more money than Imelda Marcos in a shoe store, but I figure she's worth every penny to my old libido. Met her one Saturday, married her the next."

The comment about grapes had made Mac cringe. He glanced at Retta's strained smile and knew he was in trouble. She looked at Allen in slow surprise. "You'd only known her a week?"

"Yes."

Since he seemed to enjoy volunteering personal information, she asked, "How old was this grape when you and she got married?"

He laughed heartily. "Twenty-six. And I was fifty-six. I like nice round figures." He paused for effect, his eyes twinkling. "And boy has she got one. About two hundred pounds worth."

"You must have had a very romantic courtship," Retta said in a toneless voice. "It must have been love at first sight."

"It was something at first sight. She came home with me the day we met, and never left. We're going to have a baby soon. It ought to fit in with my grandkids really well."

"That's sweet," Retta offered. Envy and frustration and humiliation twined together inside her like choking vines. No two people on earth loved each other more than she and Mac did. If he'd asked her to marry him at Disney World, she would have—wearing a silly Mouseketeer hat, if he'd asked her to do that, too. Disney World had been eight long weeks ago.

He hadn't asked then, and he still didn't ask. He never mentioned marriage, or even the prospect of their living together. It wasn't fair. And she had too much pride to ask first.

"Well, toodaloo," Allen said. "I've got to sober up and go consult on a twisted colon. Geez, I've been too busy lately."

Mac responded dryly. "I hope you get caught up with your work. And in your work."

Guffawing at the joke, Allen bounced away. Mac hung his head for a moment, then looked over at Retta. She stared fixedly at her broken club.

"I'm going to buy you a new set of clubs for your birthday," he said. "Let's get the hell out of here and go to the pro shop."

"My birthday isn't until October," she replied stiffly.

"Then they'll be an early birthday present." He was

mad because Retta was mad at him, and it hurt. He was mad at Allen, mad at the disapproving women.

He'd noticed on more than one occasion how they smiled in patronizing wonder at Retta's quaint tailored shorts and prim white blouses, her battered old golf bag and outdated clubs. They knew she could outplay any of them any day, even with her antique gear, Mac thought with pride.

Her head came up and their eyes met. He felt the full force of her dignified wrath.

"You called me a grape?" she asked coolly. "You made fun of me in front of that . . . that proctologist?"

"I don't quite remember what was said. It was a long time ago. You and I'd just met. I wasn't making fun of you, I was making fun of him for liking younger women. As you can easily figure out, I've changed my opinion of younger women considerably since then."

But what about younger women as wives? she fiercely wanted to ask. No, she wouldn't do it. She had too much self-respect to badger him into proposing. She'd bite her tongue in two before she'd introduce the subject of marriage.

"I'll see you later, Mac." Ice could have formed on her voice. He looked down at her in grim dismay.

"What are you so upset about?" he asked tersely. "This isn't like you to get bent out of shape over something so minor."

"Maybe I'm just not as cooperative and . . . undemanding as you think. And I'm getting a headache. I'm going home."

"We don't have the kind of relationship where we stomp off in separate directions without talking," he informed her. "And you don't have a car here. How's that for logic, Mr. Spock?"

Faced with that fact, she shoved her broken club into her bag and hoisted the bag to her shoulder. "I want to leave."

"I've got no problem with that," he replied. "As long as we leave together."

He grabbed his golf bag and they walked to the DeLorean in silence. When they were seated inside, she slipped her sunglasses on and stared straight ahead.

"I'm going to buy you a pair of decent sunglasses," he muttered. "Prescription sunglasses to protect your eyes on the golf course."

"No you're not."

"Those things are scratched to hell and back."

"I don't care. We settled all discussions about you spending money on me, a long time ago."

Something terrible was happening, releasing strange tensions into the air. Mac's voice rose. "I'm damned tired of you acting foolish about my money!"

"I don't want to be dependent. I was raised to take care of myself," she said primly.

"You don't want anyone to accuse you of being a normal human being," he shot back. "You love being noble and self-sacrificing. If you let go of your austere little lifestyle, you couldn't enjoy feeling arrogant anymore. That's the core of the problem."

Retta felt her face coloring. "That's not true!" But it was true, and the realization shocked her all the way to her toes. Frustration overwhelmed her. She snatched her sunglasses off and looked him squarely in the eyes. "I just don't take extravagant presents from my boyfriends."

He seethed. She'd never seen him so upset before. "First of all," he said in a tight, low voice, "I'm not your 'boyfriend,' I'm a grown man who happens to be your lover and your friend, or your 'significant other,' or whatever the hell you want to call it. Second, giving you gifts would make me happy. You hurt me, dammit. You insult me by acting so righteously narrow-minded."

Retta wavered, her innate honesty forcing her to consider all the truth behind his accusations. She started to apologize just as Mac threw out his hands in a frustrated, sarcastic gesture.

"Retta, if we were married you'd take my money. What's the difference?" His voice rose again. "Do I have to marry you to be good to you?"

Oh, that did it. So he thought of marriage as a forced option, did he? "No!" she threw back. "You don't have to do anything but take me back to the condominium so I can get in my austere, noble little car and go back to my austere, noble little apartment where I can be austere and noble alone!"

"Terrific!"

She jabbed the sunglasses back over her eyes and sank deep into the seat, her hands clenched together. He punched a button that turned the radio on full blast. The DeLorean's tires squealed as Mac slung it down the drive toward the club's massive gate. Retta noted with grim satisfaction that club members out strolling on the lawns pointed at the car and gave Mac dirty looks.

Neither of them said a word during the thirty-minute drive back to the Gold Shore condos. Mac jerked the De-Lorean into his reserved parking space in the building's garage and cut the engine.

"Good-bye," she said immediately and got out. Her anger had faded to stricken weariness. This was awful. They'd never fought like this before, they'd hardly even exchanged a quarrelsome word. He walked around to her side of the car as she began tugging at her golf bag.

"Retta, don't," he said hoarsely. She couldn't look at him, or she'd crumble into a million undignified pieces.

"Please," she whispered. "Just let me go."

"You don't want to go, dammit. I don't want you to go." She stopped moving and stood with her head bowed. He slid his hand around her arm. His voice was bittersweet.

"If you're going to be noble and austere, then come do it at my place." He tried to joke. "I'll just force myself not to watch."

She stood up and looked at him with troubled, tired eyes and a fully developed headache. Then she nodded. He shut the car's winglike door and they walked quietly inside the building, his hand still on her arm.

When they reached his condo she walked in ahead of him and went straight to the master bath to find a bottle of aspirin. He walked in behind her as she swallowed two tablets, and they shared a look that conveyed tense sorrow. Still not speaking, he went to the big, sunken tub, closed the drain, and turned on the faucet.

"Get undressed," he said simply. "We're going to make love to each other."

She turned and watched as he disappeared out the bathroom door. Because she knew Mac's sensitive concept of making love, she knew that he wasn't referring primarily to sex. They often made love for hours, and the physical joinings were only brief interludes of intensity in the midst of it.

Retta sighed, feeling confused by her mixture of sensual feelings and depression. She stripped off her golf shoes along with the neatly pressed, tailored blue shorts and simple white top.

Mac came back with a handful of short candles. He stopped and let his gaze filter slowly over her, taking in the frilly white bra and panties she still wore.

"All of it," he instructed. He put the candles around the tub, lit them, then retrieved a bottle of perfumed bath oil she'd brought him. Retta dropped her underwear onto the room's cool ocher tiles. He knelt with his back to her, turning off the faucet, and she stood naked, watching him.

He glanced over his shoulder. "Come here and get in the tub."

She walked past him like an obedient slave, her gaze straight ahead, and stepped into the warm, fragrant water. She sat down as he went to a wall plate and switched off the lights. Retta felt the pit of her stomach drop as Mac loomed above her in the dim, glowing candlelight.

He was already barefoot. He removed his tan shorts and white golf shirt slowly, dropping them to the floor without looking. His eyes stayed on her face. He wore only a jock strap now, and with a quick push from his finger it slid to the tiled floor, too. He stepped out of it and into the tub.

Retta felt mesmerized as he sank down in the water, facing her, and held out his arms. She made a soft, sad sound and slid forward to be enclosed in an undemanding, tender embrace that offered silent healing. With her legs around his waist and her arms around his neck, she cupped smooth water in her hand and dampened his shoulder, then rested her cheek there.

He cupped water over her back and shoulders, then nestled his face into her hair. They sat still except for their stroking, wet hands, which moved so gently that the water made very little sound as they scooped it up.

Several minutes passed before she relaxed enough to let silent tears roll down her cheeks onto his gleaming shoulder. He felt them and hugged her tighter.

"Head feel better?" Mac asked.

"Uh-huh."

"I love you," he whispered raggedly. "I think I knew that I loved you even when I called you a grape."

She was still crying, but now she managed to smile. "You can buy me a new set of golf clubs, Mac. And sunglasses. I am insufferably arrogant."

"You're not insufferably anything," he corrected. "You're just so afraid of needing anyone." His voice dropped. "I want you to need me. In every way."

In every way but marriage? she asked silently. Retta gritted her teeth and sternly instructed herself not to dwell on that disruptive question anymore. Be thankful for this incredible man, she told herself. Just be thankful.

They nuzzled each other, moving their mouths closer by slow inches, until the nuzzling became an erotic kiss. When she felt his body respond she simply raised herself and took him in, rocking on his lap while the glowing pool of water undulated around them.

"The water's making love to me," he murmured. "You've put magic in it." His mouth pulled gently on the sensitive skin of her throat while his careful fingertips pinched the hard peaks of her breasts.

Retta dimly heard him through a pleasant mist of sensation, and she shut her eyes tightly as he pushed even deeper inside her. "Amadeus, I never . . . want to fight with you again," she managed with a small, spare breath. "But reconciliation is . . . oh . . . Mac . . ."

"Fantastic," he supplied gruffly.

They moved in unison like two finely meshed parts in an exquisite machine. She rested her cheek against his forehead and felt his damp, soft hair tickling her. The flame of a nearby candle hypnotized her. She was like that flame, hot and steady, rising, grabbing at the air, flickering as the air became too thin, climbing . . .

And at the searing pinnacle she heard Mac's voice telling her she was the sweetest sight his eyes could ever beg to see, that he was coming home to her, to wait for him, to wait, yes, he felt her smile on his mouth, why was she smiling when he just needed one . . . more . . . kiss . . . yes, like that . . . yesss.

They curled up together in the shoulder-deep water and soaked, tangled like marionettes who'd just finished a joyous dance. Retta took a soft sponge from the tub's rim, soaked it, and lightly scrubbed both her body and his. They had loved away the awful tension between them; now they nurtured the new peace.

Mac closed his eyes and let his head droop back against the tub's edge. His fingers followed the course of the sponge as she trailed it down his stomach.

"Are you sure you aren't a geisha in disguise?" he quipped softly. "You serve me so well." She smiled wickedly and put extra pressure on the sponge just as it reached his thighs. "Oooh . . . oooh . . . ouch . . . stop . . . you're not a geisha, you're a gremlin!"

"No, I'm a piranha!"

Growling in delight, she ducked her head under the water and attacked his rump with nipping teeth. He nearly choked on laughter as he shoved at her and flailed his arms.

He sank under beside her and pulled her on top of him, then wrapped his long arms and legs around her, pinning her helplessly to him. Water sloshed everywhere as he shoved his body into a sitting position. Giggling and gasping, Retta found herself mashed against him from shoulder to ankle, her arms trapped, her breasts flat against his chest. By craning her head back she could look him straight in the face.

"What are you?" she asked tartly. "A sea serpent?"

He shook his head, pursed his lips, and launched a long stream of oily water directly into her face. She squealed with helpless laughter.

"I," he said solemnly, "am an octopus. And octopi spit."

They were still wrestling and chuckling when they heard the muted rattle of the condo door opening. Mac sat bolt upright and held out one hand toward her in a silencing gesture.

"What the—" he said tersely.

"Dad!" a deep, friendly voice boomed from the living room. "It's your long-lost college-age brat, come for a surprise visit!"

Retta's amused gasp was followed by the stunned realization that Lucas McHale was headed straight for the master bath.

CHAPTER TEN

SHE HEARD THE combination of dismay and laughter in Mac's startled expletive as he leaped out of the tub and snatched a large white towel from the brass rack by the door.

"What do you want me to do, Amadeus?" she whispered loudly. "Pretend I'm a very conscientious cleaning lady? I can hide . . ."

"I'm not ashamed of you!" he whispered back fervently. "I told Lucas about you weeks ago. It's just . . . he's never seen . . . the idea of me, his dad . . ."

"I think I'd better drown myself," she said wryly.

"Don't you dare drown and leave me to explain this alone," he quipped. "Get dressed and come on out."

"Dad!" the hearty male voice called again. "You old solitary reprobate! I'm here!"

The voice was at the bedroom door. Retta caught a glimpse of blond hair just before she sank down in the tub with her arms over her chest. Mac held the towel around his dripping body, stepped out of the bathroom with a quick show of jaunty aplomb, and gracefully slammed the door behind him.

She heard their muffled conversation, but couldn't decipher the words. Only two of the tubside candles had escaped being soaked, and Retta found herself alone in an eerily dark place. Her teasing attitude faded as she wondered what Lucas McHale would think as soon as he realized that his father hadn't been taking a bath alone.

"Damn, damn," she said hoarsely. Retta could dimly hear voices on the other side of the door. She quickly got out of the tub, flicked on the light, and began dressing. Of course Lucas would be hurt and defensive—he'd resent her for having such a . . . a carnal effect on Mac. He'd resent her young age, her implied assumption of his mother's role, the way she divided Mac's affections.

"Please, Lucas, just give me a chance," she pleaded under her breath. "I love him as much as you do. Please."

Her hair was not only wet, it was slick with bath oil. Retta stared at the waif with wrinkled clothes and matted hair inside the teakwood rectangle of a huge mirror over the vanity, and decided that she didn't look threatening, at least.

She looked pitiful. Maybe Lucas would feel sorry for her, as if she were an ugly kitten. Oh, Dad, he'd say. Don't take her to the humane society. Just clean her up a little and let her stay. Retta clucked her tongue in self-rebuke at her nervous whimsy, then wrapped a white towel around her head. She put one hand on the doorknob and listened. Mac and Lucas had left the room.

Her heart racing, Retta opened the door and walked barefoot into the casual elegance of Mac's bedroom. Her ears strained toward the hallway door, and she heard low male laughter and conversation from somewhere in the living room. Laughter? Retta squared her shoulders and stalked toward the sound.

". . . and I'm so proud of you, Dad! I'm so relieved that you're not alone anymore! You don't have to explain!"

"I just don't want you to think badly of Retta . . ."

"Dad, any woman who can get you to play water wiggle has my vote of approval."

Retta's mouth dropped open in relief and amusement. She heard Mac's blustery, "Water wiggle?"

She stopped just inside the living room and watched as a handsome man—not a boy, because even at twenty-one there was something sophisticated and mature about Lucas McHale's face—gave Mac an affectionate hug.

Lucas wasn't quite as tall as Mac, but slightly heavier, with a physique that hinted at bodybuilding. He wore jogging shoes, faded jeans, and a Northwestern University T-shirt. Mac, thank goodness, had located a black terrycloth robe.

"Dad, I didn't mean to embarrass you," Lucas said, choking on repressed laughter.

"I'm a doctor. Nothing embarrasses me," Mac answered dryly. He paused. "Water wiggle?"

Lucas caught sight of her and turned friendly blue eyes in her direction. Despite their warmth, those sharp eyes assessed her from toe to head with merciless attention to detail. She crossed her hands gracefully, lifted her chin, and let him look. Go ahead. I know you want to judge me, she told him silently. Mac swiveled around and saw her.

"Retta, I want you to meet my son, Lucas," he said softly. "Lucas, this is Retta Stanton. A very special lady." Mac smiled at her so tenderly that she almost forgot Lucas was there. The corner of Mac's mouth crooked up. "When you really want to get her attention, call her Henrietta."

"Henrietta," Lucas said in a warm voice that was disarmingly familiar, then extended his hand. She crossed the room and grasped it firmly. They shook with a strong, quick motion.

His brawny, blond good looks were very different from Mac's leaner and darker features, Retta mused. She saw Judith McHale's Scandinavian beauty in Lucas, but his wonderful voice and the warmth in his blue eyes could only be Mac's gift. She silently rebuked herself for not expecting Mac's son to be gracious and loving.

Retta took the towel off her head and draped it over her arm with a grand show of dignity. She looked at Mac and found relief and humor in his eyes.

"He's on to us, isn't he?" she asked solemnly. "He knows I'm not the maid."

Lucas laughed and nodded. "And I'm thrilled. When

Dad mentioned he was seeing someone, he was pretty mysterious about specifics."

Retta gave Mac a teasing look. "He didn't say he was dating a grape, did he?"

"No." Lucas looked at his father with intrigue, and Mac cleared his throat.

"I told Lucas that I'd found someone very mature and very intelligent."

Lucas interjected, "I thought, 'Oh, no, Dad's starting to sound middle-aged. She probably wears support hose.'" He gazed at Mac devilishly. "But I should have known better."

Retta stiffened with slight chagrin. She wore support hose and loved them. "Lucas, I think you ought to understand about me." He swiveled his gaze back, looking a little worried by her warning tone of voice.

Mac watched her with a wry smile. He already suspected what his frank, honest darling was going to say next.

"Yes?" Lucas asked. Retta took a deep breath.

"I'm only five years older than you. I'm sixteen years younger than Mac. He's been very conscious of that fact. I want you to know that he didn't chase me, I chased him. And I want you to know that I don't have a father complex and I'm not after his money."

"Whew!" Lucas's eyes gleamed with amusement, and Retta began to frown. He turned to Mac. "You were right, Dad. She is quaint!"

"Quaint?" she echoed with sharp undertones, eyeing Mac.

"His word, his word," Mac interjected quickly, pointing at Lucas and chuckling. "Not mine. I said you were old-fashioned. Charming. Charming and old-fashioned."

"Oh." She smiled, considered her image for a moment, and nodded sheepishly to Lucas. "I probably am quaint." Then she added in a more somber voice, "But I care deeply about your father, and I wouldn't do anything to hurt him. I just want you to know that."

"See what I told you, Luke?" Mac asked. "Very mature. Very intelligent."

Mac slid an arm around her waist. She looked up at him and received a gaze so loving that her throat closed with emotion. She knew Lucas was watching the two of them intently.

"Okay," Lucas said softly, almost in awe. He gave them his blessing with that simple word. "Okay."

Mad Wolf White seemed to be crushing every vertebra in The Tarantula's beefy neck. Retta nearly choked on her last bite of cheese pizza in empathy as she watched the professional wrestlers grapple with each other on television.

"He's killing him, Lucas!" she managed finally, coughing. "Even a tarantula deserves to lose with dignity. It's barbaric!"

Sitting beside her on the couch, Mac teased, "No, it's fake." He patted her back soothingly. Lucas grinned up at her from his place on the floor, and nodded.

"You want to take part in that?" she asked him, wide-eyed. "What about your degree in social science? Mac said after you graduate you want to work with juvenile delinquents."

"But that's also why I want to wrestle for a few years," Lucas said jovially. He pointed at the TV screen. "Have you ever seen so many grown juvenile delinquents in your life? Think of what I'll learn!"

They all laughed. The program ended and Mac clicked a button on the TV's remote control. The screen went dark. Retta shook her head in disbelief, her eyes still curious as she studied Lucas. She turned to Mac.

"It's inherited," she said wryly. "You've given him all your eccentric genes."

Mac nodded, chuckling. Retta kissed him on the cheek, stood up, and extended a hand to Lucas.

"But I like eccentric men," she told him. "It was nice meeting you, Lucas."

He jumped up and politely shook her hand, his eyes

gleaming with never-ending hilarity at her formal ways. Retta felt much older than twenty-six, suddenly, but Lucas's teasing was gentle and she knew they could be friends. That was the only thing that mattered.

Mac, now fully dressed in blue jogging sweats and a white T-shirt, walked her downstairs to her car. They held hands and smiled at each other as they crossed the parking garage.

"Strange day," he murmured, as he gathered her to him for a good-bye kiss. "I wish you'd stay with me tonight." His mouth crooked in a wry smile. "You know what my worldly son said? When you went to the bathroom he told me, 'She *is* staying tonight, isn't she? You're not going to be a Puritan and send her home because I'm here, I hope.'"

She nuzzled her cheek against his. "I do want to stay. But you explained to Lucas, I hope, that old-fashioned, part-Polish women polka off to their own apartments under these circumstances?"

"I did," he whispered. "I won't ask you to do something that makes you feel uncomfortable."

Retta tipped her head back and made a conscious effort to keep her expression neutral. You know how we could solve this quaint little problem, don't you, Amadeus? she thought sadly. We could get married.

But to him she only said, "I'll look forward to brunch tomorrow. Lucas is a great guy."

Mac hugged her tightly. She felt his breath against her ear, then his lips. "Lucas is driving back to campus right after brunch. Then you and I'll make a Sunday-afternoon shopping trip."

"For what?" she murmured, lost in the cozy sensations his embrace generated.

"For your new golf gear. For new sunglasses. For a lot of things."

She started to protest, but he quickly angled his face toward hers and covered her mouth with a kiss. He waited long enough to muddle her train of thought before he trailed the kiss across her cheek.

"You gave in, remember?" he chided. "You're going to let me enjoy buying things for you. Right?"

"Oh. Right," she said lightly. "I better go home and relish being austere one last night."

Chuckling, he held the car door while she got inside. As was usual whenever she left to go anywhere alone, he didn't turn back toward the garage-level elevator until he'd watched her drive out of sight. Be careful, he always told her silently. Drive safely. Hurry back. I love you. Then, his head down in thought, he headed for the elevator.

Lucas was drinking a beer at the kitchen's breakfast bar. Low light from the stained-glass lamp over the bar gave the kitchen a shadowy, brooding atmosphere. Mac sat down across from Lucas and noted the same attitude in his eyes.

"Aha," Mac said slowly, while something tense and expectant coiled inside him. Somehow, he'd known there were reservations under the friendly facade Lucas presented to Retta. "Okay, mister," Mac ordered. "Talk. What could you possibly dislike about Retta?"

"Nothing." Lucas shook his head, obviously surprised at the question. Mac frowned, feeling bewildered.

"Then what is it?"

"It's you," Lucas said tautly. "I'm disappointed in you."

"Why, for God's sake?"

Lucas pointed an accusing finger at him. "You ought to marry her, Dad, or you ought to let her go. She's crazy about you. You're being selfish and cruel. That stinks."

Determination raced through Mac's veins like poison. So that was it.

"I'm not being selfish, son," Mac answered tightly. "I'm being unselfish."

"You let yourself fall in love with her, you let her fall in love with you, and you won't take the commitment any further?" Lucas shook his head again. "I'll never understand how you can be so damned principled for no good reason."

"I'm not going to tie her to me. I'm not going to tie anyone to me."

Lucas nearly yelled at him. "What in the hell do you

think you've done already? She loves you. You love her. Isn't that a tie?"

Mac nodded, his expression rigid with control. "But it's not a legal entanglement for her. If anything should happen to me—accident, illness, whatever—she wouldn't be responsible. You'd be responsible, unfortunately. I don't even want you involved, but I can't do much about it, since you're my next of kin."

"You're so cold about it." Lucas crushed the beer can into the bar's wooden surface. "So clinical."

Mac felt as if each of the next words ground inches off his teeth. "I will not be a burden to anyone if I can help it," he said with lethal emphasis. "I know what I'm doing."

"Mom wouldn't want it this way," Lucas persisted. "She wouldn't want you to live your life alone, being so freaking noble."

"I'm not alone. I've got Retta and you." Mac felt pressure banging against his temple. I'm getting one of Retta's tension headaches, he thought. One of Retta's . . . was she that much a part of him, that he thought of her pain as an entity he automatically shared? He inhaled raggedly. If he had to, could he live without her? Yes, yes, by God, he could, he told himself.

"Have you ever mentioned to Retta that you don't intend to remarry?" Lucas demanded.

"No. She's never asked."

"She will. I'd say she's waiting for you to make the first move."

"I know. One day I'll tell her how I feel." Mac added silently, one day I'll tell her, when I can bear to watch the disappointment and pain come into her expression, when I can bear to risk losing her. He gazed at Lucas through narrowed eyes. "That's all I intend to say about this subject tonight."

Lucas stood up and slung the beer can into a trash container. "Some cardiologist you are," he said coldly. "Check out your own heart, man. See if it's still there." He left the kitchen and a few seconds later Mac heard one of the guest room doors slam.

Mac pounded a fist against the bar's top. In the course of one day, good old mellow, easygoing Dr. McHale had managed to fight with the only two people he loved. Feeling miserable, he went into the garden room and stared blankly at the dark expanse of Lake Michigan and the shimmering lights of the tall buildings along Chicago's shoreline.

So Lucas accused him of being heartless. What was it the Tin Man said when Dorothy was about to leave Oz forever? "I know I have a heart, because right now I feel it breaking in two?" Mac smiled coldly at the melodramatic words. They had never seemed more appropriate.

"Oh, Amadeus." Retta shook her head. "I feel funny."

"You look marvelous." Mac squinted at her in the bright July sun and put his best Billy Crystal imitation into the word. "Maaah-vel-ous!" She couldn't help laughing, buoyed by the almost manic enthusiasm that seemed to pervade everything they did these days.

After Lucas left on Sunday they'd gone shopping—no, not shopping, spending, she corrected. If she so much as glanced at something with more than mild appreciation, Mac bought it. A powder blue golf bag, a set of the best clubs, the promised sunglasses, then clothes, shoes, lingerie, books, records.

It was insane, embarrassing, and finally, delightful. She'd never expected to feel so . . . so free to be sinfully indulgent. Mac encouraged her, he insisted that she splurge. When they'd settled into the DeLorean for the last time, with boxes and bags stuffed all around them, even filling her lap, Mac had reached into his lollipop bag and handed her a chocolate sucker.

It was too much, coming on top of all the presents, and she burst into tears that surprised her as much as they unnerved him. She was a child again, and her Santa Claus had beautiful blue eyes and a sympathetic shoulder into which she cried about all sorts of whimsical little dreams that had just come true.

Now she looked down at her new shorts and wondered

if she hadn't been mistaken about some of those dreams. This was a nightmare.

"We can't go out on the course dressed like this," she protested. "I'm changing my mind. I'm chickening out. I want my old tailored shorts and white shirt back."

"Forget it," he said firmly, and took her hand. "We're a matched set." They walked along, their golf bags clanking against their shoulders.

"Like plastic flamingoes," she noted. "Too ugly to appeal to anything but each other."

He only laughed, and Retta watched him with gleaming eyes. If any man could make baggy, Hawaiian-print Jams look sexy, Mac could. The shorts were unstructured and nearly knee length. With them he wore a golf shirt of the most potent aquamarine she'd ever seen in her life. It was almost as potent as the screaming pink of her tank top. Almost as potent as the chartreuse print of her own baggy shorts.

"Good afternoon," Mac called to a group of club members on the driving range.

"Good afternoon," Retta echoed. She'd never let Mac know that she felt uncomfortable around these people, some of whom hadn't been particularly friendly to her.

Especially Jean Conway, who kept bringing up the subject of Isabella Edwards as if Retta had somehow ruined a wonderful plan. Retta had known for a long time that a few of the women considered her and her old golf clubs to be intruders. Now they couldn't hide their amazed interest in the colorful new Retta Stanton and friend.

"Where's the luau, Mac?" one man called, laughing.

"Put a label on it and call it fruit punch!" another chortled.

"Fruit, that's it!" someone else yelled. "It's Carmen Miranda with hairy legs!"

"Envy!" Mac yelled back cheerfully. "Jealousy! None of you bums has legs good enough to show off this way! Even dressed like this, Retta and I can whip any of you with twenty strokes to spare! We make a great team! A great team!"

"Mac, Mac," she whispered fervently, blushing from all the boisterous attention they were receiving. "What's gotten into you?" He was almost daring people to stare at him.

He looked at her with a haunting intensity in his eyes. "We're good together, no matter what, Retta. We know how to enjoy the moment, to enjoy life, to have a wonderful time." Suddenly he seemed angry. "I won't let anyone or anything take this time away from us. I won't, dammit."

"What's wrong?" she asked, puzzled and worried.

"Nothing." He faced the other club members again. "Come on! Who's brave enough to play a little 'Skins' with us! Proceeds go to the winner's favorite charity!"

There were whoops and yells. "Okay, you cocky son-ofagun! Get your money out! I'll play! Me, too!" A small army of energized golfers started trudging toward them. Mac grinned like a valiant man who enjoyed fighting the most when defeat was imminent. Retta looked at him in alarm. Something strange was going on inside her beloved Amadeus, and she had to find out what.

But she didn't. Not that afternoon, when they won fifty but lost two hundred dollars due to his competitive frenzy, and not over the next few days, when their mutual workloads kept them apart.

On the following Saturday morning their standard golf game ended almost before it began when Mac had to leave and perform an emergency surgery. That night they had to go to the Conways' house to attend a birthday party for an old friend of Mac's.

Mac was supposed to pick her up. He arrived at her apartment thirty minutes late, his tie in his hand, his hair half-brushed, circles of fatigue under his eyes.

"I was getting worried," she told him as she opened the door.

"Dammit, I'm sorry," he snapped. After a moment of shock, she saw the apology bleed into his eyes. "Retta, I . . ." he added hoarsely.

"Amadeus, sshhh." She drew him inside and hugged

him. "You need some friendly rejuvenation before you go anywhere else."

"I do," he answered in a low, tired voice. She took him back to her bedroom and guided him down on his back atop her blue coverlet. Tenderness for him overwhelmed her as she slipped out of her hose and panties while he watched with quiet desire in his eyes.

She unfastened his clothes until she had just enough access to tantalize his body, then she spread herself and the flowing skirt of her sundress over his thighs and gently loved him.

She lay on his chest for a long time afterwards, cuddled in his arms, listening with a rapt little smile while he told her precisely how good she made him feel.

"Can we skip the party and just stay here?" she asked softly. They had to talk, she had to learn why he had so much tension inside him these days.

"And miss showing you off in this sexy white sundress?" he countered, smiling. "No way." His voice grew more somber. "And I'd really feel like a heel if we didn't put in an appearance. I've already been a heel once tonight. Forgive me. That surgery was a hell of a strain."

"I understand, my wonderful sick-ticker tinkerer," she teased immediately, and kissed him. Retta sensed that he needed her cheerful cooperation desperately, and she gave it to him now with a smile as she began straightening his clothes.

The party was enormous. It was in an enormous house with an enormous swimming pool and most of the women in attendance were wearing enormous diamonds. But Retta didn't care. She'd adjusted to luxury now—and even acknowledged the fact that in a sundress she enjoyed drawing unabashed stares from men.

Mac got a shot of bourbon and joined a group of physicians in the living room discussing the Jarvik-7 artificial heart. Retta wandered around quietly, sipping her usual Tom Collins and smiling at whoever caught her eye.

"Well, hello there," a friendly female voice gushed. Retta turned a polite gaze to Jean Conway.

"Hello." Matchmaking twit, she added silently. You'd still like to pair up one of your older friends with Mac, wouldn't you? The woman who looked back at her was much like Isabella—stylish and beautiful and graceful. But Jean had long red hair instead of blond, and she wasn't particularly tall. In fact, she was a pint-sized china doll in a green dress of raw silk.

"Would you settle a bet for me?" Jean asked.

"Certainly."

"Someone at the club said the other day that your background is Amish. I said not."

"Why would anyone think I'm Amish?" Retta asked innocently. "Do I look . . ." Her voice trailed off. Plain. Up until recently she'd looked very plain, and that was the intent this remark was meant to convey. For just one second she felt hurt and angry.

Then she glanced over at Mac, and inspiration came to her. The old Retta would have turned into an icy clam. She would have revealed just how vulnerable this woman's silliness made her feel. But not the new Retta. Oh, what she'd learned from Mac about grace under pressure! She bluffed.

"Why yes, I'm from an Amish family in Wisconsin!" Retta said cheerfully, and smiled. Jean's eyes narrowed shrewdly, but Retta only smiled with increasing delight.

She hooked her arm through Jean's and leaned toward her to speak in a companionable whisper. "As you can see, I don't live by the Amish traditions right now, because Mac's a little uncomfortable with the idea." She gestured toward her chin and looked solemn. "If we were to be married and go back to the farm, he'd have to grow one of those lovely long beards the Amish men wear. And his would be all gray. He's not really keen on the idea of having a gray beard. He says he'd look like a fuzzy old hillbilly."

Jean looked at her with startled eyes that indicated tentative belief. "Really?" she asked.

"Really," Retta said and nodded.

"Then Mac's changed his mind about remarrying?"

Retta never let her expression change, but she was aware of her hands growing cold and her stomach dropping with a sick sensation. Changed his mind? "Oh, we've talked about it a little."

"If you've gotten him to relent on that subject, I give you credit," Jean said with a blunt nod. "I've had a half dozen women tell me the man's a hopeless loner who'll never stop mourning for Judith."

"Well . . ." Retta found she had almost no resources for keeping up this nonchalant show. She wanted to take Jean by the shoulders and say, "Do you mean he doesn't intend to remarry? Is that what he's said to everyone?" Another part of Retta's mind kept reminding her, "What he's said about other women couldn't apply to me." She shut her jumbled emotions away and kept the calm, smiling expression on her face. "He's relenting a little. Tell me what the walking wounded have reported from their battles."

Jean nodded again. "Come on, Amish. I think I like you. Let's go discuss this loner of yours."

She tugged on her arm and they walked toward the privacy of a corner. Then Jean began to talk.

CHAPTER ELEVEN

"HAVE YOU SEEN Retta lately?" Mac asked Allen. He tried to sound casual, but the fact that his thorough search of the party-packed house hadn't turned up any sign of her was beginning to alarm him. He'd gotten caught up in the discussion about the Jarvik-7, and when he'd looked at his watch nearly an hour had passed.

"Sure." Allen waved a pudgy hand filled with a martini glass toward the wide hallway that led to the home's manicured backyard and pool area. "She's in the pool house with a bunch of other people. They've got a jukebox cranked up. Last time I saw her she was teaching some guy how to polka."

Mac grinned and ambled out of the house like the picture of unhurried calm. Inside he was thinking, I'm the only man she's supposed to polka with, dammit. He felt ridiculous for feeling jealous, but couldn't help himself.

The pool house would make a nice home for a family of four, Mac thought drolly as he crossed the lawn. A set of double doors opened onto a wide deck. Music and light and laughter poured out of a recreation room complete with a fully stocked bar and a billiard table.

And Retta was the center of attention.

Mac stopped on the edge of the crowd, smiling while the whimsical jealousy inside him became an unexpected monster. She was waltzing—to the "Blue Danube," for

God's sake—with a tall, handsome kid who couldn't be more than twenty years old. But the kid looked like a young Ryan O'Neal, and he had a knowing little smile. He also had his arms around her back. Worse yet, she had her arms around his shoulders and her smile seemed to be telling him that she knew what he was thinking and found it flattering.

The kid could waltz like a pro. He wore a white polo shirt over his very tanned torso, and stylish white slacks on his very long legs. White moccasins encased his bare feet.

Sockless bum, Mac thought. He'd never considered himself capable of such adolescent jealousy until this moment, watching Retta in the arms of a boy not very many years past adolescence.

When the song ended, everyone applauded. The kid hugged Retta and then, to Mac's utter amazement, bent down and gave her a light kiss on the lips. The surprise was evident on her face, but so was the hint of pleasure. She glanced away in a manner that seemed almost guilty to Mac, and her eyes found him in the crowd. She winked coyly.

The flippant gesture annoyed him, but he arranged a grin on his face and nodded, then made himself applaud along with the others. All right, honey, I'm being a turnip-headed ogre, he told her silently. The kid's cute. Now pat him on the head and come over here to your full-grown man.

But a slow Streisand song floated out of the jukebox and she kept her arms around the young Ryan O'Neal's shoulders. Mac stood in motionless shock and watched the two of them sway to the music. Their bodies weren't touching, but they might as well have been. The kid was talking to her, and she kept her dark hazel eyes trained on his face in apparent interest.

Mac forced his taut muscles into a semblance of a nonchalant stride as he wound his way through the crowded room toward her. Dear God, something was terribly wrong. Retta would never deliberately provoke him this way, otherwise.

"Excuse me," he told the young man, with a jovial smile. "I'm cutting in on your action."

"Hi, Mac," Retta said lightly. She looked over at him as she and her partner came to a halt. "This is Justin Richards. He's a friend of the Conways' son."

"Bronson McHale," Mac offered, and held out a hand. With great aplomb, Justin shook it, and grinned.

"I stole your girl," he said cheerfully. The kid had dimples on either side of his mouth, Mac noted.

"Give her back," Mac answered just as cheerfully. Before I deepen your dimples with my fist, he added inside.

Justin stepped away, smiling. He squeezed Retta's hand and Mac noticed the sweet smile she bestowed in return. "Catch you on the flip side, lady," Justin told her.

Then he was gone, and Mac faced her alone. He frowned as she put her arms around his neck and managed to look completely innocent. "So do your duty, Mac. Finish my dance."

Retta gasped when he jerked her tight against him, his hands like a vise on her lower back. They moved slowly to the music without hearing a note of it. Mac saw sadness and anger in her startled, unguarded expression. Now he'd get to the bottom of her completely outrageous and completely uncharacteristic behavior.

"Tell me what's wrong," he commanded simply, his voice hard. "And do it quick."

She shook her head, her mouth a firm line of resistance. "Not here."

"You name the place, then."

"Are you ready to go home? I don't want to ruin the party for you."

Anxiety made a knot inside his stomach. What did she intend to say? "Retta, after the way you taunted me with that kid I'm ready to pull my damned hair out. The party's over. Come on."

She started to protest his accusation, but stopped when she saw the warning look in his eyes. All right, she was very upset, and she had been taunting him a little. Retta nodded grimly.

Five minutes later, after quick good-byes, they settled
into the DeLorean's intimate confines. The cover of summer darkness gave her carefully controlled smile a respite,
and she let misery weigh it down. Mac immediately leaned
toward her, clasping one hand on the top of the passenger
seat and the other on the dash as if he intended to trap her
on her side of the car.

"Talk," he ordered.

She sighed wearily. "You want me to be my usual
bluntly honest self?"

"You got it, Retta."

She took a moment to gather words, the muscles in her
jaw flexing with restraint. "Why didn't you tell me that
you never want to marry again? Why did I have to hear it
from Jean Conway tonight?"

The aggression drained out of him. Mac sat back in his
seat and rubbed one hand to his forehead in a gesture that
conveyed his own weariness, and defeat. The time had
come to face the music. The waltz, rather. How ironic, he
thought bitterly. He didn't answer for a moment.

"Because I'm a selfish bastard and I figured that you'd
feel less enthusiastic about me as soon as you knew," he
admitted in a leaden voice. "Because I don't want to lose
you, but I don't want to tie you to me, either."

Her voice hit him with low, controlled fury. "So we're
back to the old problem. You still intend to die alone some-
day, without being a burden to anyone." She tossed her
head. "And you had the nerve to chide me the other day for
being noble and arrogant. How dare you." Her voice
shook. "How dare you . . . insult my feelings for you by
shutting me out of your future."

"I love you," he said hoarsely, his voice a mere whisper. Mac knotted a hand around the DeLorean's steering
wheel as if he needed support. But even in the dim light,
his gaze seared her with its unyielding strength. "But I'll
never ask you to stay with me the rest of my life."

She clenched her hands into fists and sank them deep
into her lap to keep from pounding the car's sleek dashboard in frustration. "What were you going to do, Mac?"

She wouldn't have believed she could put such harsh cynicism in her voice. "Sleep with me a few years, then pat me on the head and send me off to find someone new?"

Mac made a taut, angry sound in the back of his throat and snatched her hands into his. His fingers bit into her fists, forced them to open, then wound between her fingers in a powerful hold.

"Don't degrade what we've shared with accusations like that. I may be a selfish bastard, but I'm not a cold-hearted one. I didn't want to think about the future. I just wanted to enjoy all the happiness you brought me, all the happiness I never thought I'd let myself have again . . ."

"All the happiness you could have for the rest of your life, Mac."

"No! I want you to find someone younger, someone who hasn't been hurt so badly—someone who can stand the risk of being torn to hell and back if anything happened to you . . ."

He stopped abruptly. Retta was stunned.

"Now I see," she said in a voice full of wonder. "You're not really afraid that you'll be a burden to someone who loves you. You're afraid that someone you love will die. And after losing Judith, you couldn't stand that again, could you?"

After a heartrending second he nodded. Mac released her hands. His magnificent voice was a shell of itself. "That's right." He shook his head in weary exasperation at her insight. "All right, that's the truth. Maybe I didn't want to recognize it, before."

Bittersweet sympathy did to her what anger had not. Tears ran down her cheeks as she slumped back in the DeLorean's plush seat and simply looked at his bowed head.

"Mac," she said in a pleading voice, "I can't promise you that I won't die." She took a deep breath. "But I can promise you that I'll love you at least as long as I live." He shivered visibly. "And I'll give you children who'll love you just as much as I do."

"Dear God," he said weakly. "Children." Mac faced

forward, closed his eyes, and let his head rest back against the driver's seat.

"Now I'm asking for the impossible, I suppose," she said in a tired voice. "I just assumed you loved children. Especially after I saw how close you and Lucas are."

"I do love children." He cleared his throat. "I just never considered the possibility of having any more of my own."

"Consider it," she begged softly. He turned his head and looked at her for a long, brooding moment. She knew he was going to shake his head even before he began to do it.

"I'd probably be the oldest father at Little League, Retta. The oldest father at ballet recitals. The oldest father . . ."

"I understand." Her voice was soaked in disappointment. "You don't have to explain your age fixation to me again. It's an impenetrable shield around you. I thought I'd broken through, but I was wrong." She faced forward, too, then pressed her fingertips into her temples as if she might suddenly fall apart. Her voice broke. "God! I've been wrong about so many things!"

"Retta, don't . . ."

"So." She put her hands in her lap, straightened her back, and stared numbly ahead. Her tone was the essence of controlled sorrow. "We're left with a simple decision, Amadeus." She paused, and he heard her inhale raggedly. "Should we end this affair before it becomes even more complicated?"

Mac closed his eyes. Let her go, he told himself in the same vicious inner voice he'd used so long ago, right after they'd met. But he couldn't speak the words now any more than he could then.

"I think," she said softly, and he heard faint choking sounds, "that the answer is yes. And I think . . . I have to be the one to say good-bye first."

"Not tonight. Not like this."

She looked at him with grim humor in her eyes. "Do you think waiting would make it easier?"

His face ashen, Mac reached over and grasped her shoulders. She turned to face him, her body stiff. "I have no honor at all," he said curtly. "Not where you're concerned. Don't leave me. Let's go on the way we have been. By God, if you think I've been good to you before, just wait until you see what I do in the future. We'll . . ."

But she was already shaking her head, shaking it slowly, as if she were in such pain that she no longer knew what she was doing. "I've got some painful memories of my own, Mac. Not as sad as yours but . . . I made a fool of myself over someone once before . . . hoping, waiting, trying so hard to be everything he wanted because I thought I could win him over. I couldn't." She shuddered. "I can't bear to be hurt like that again."

They looked at each other in silent despair. Finally he reached up with both hands and caressed the tears off her cheeks. She put her fingertips on his face in the same way and he realized that he had tears there, too.

"I'm going to go back in the house," she said softly. "And I'm going to call a taxi."

"No," he asked hoarsely.

She touched a finger to his lips in gentle rebuke. "Yes. That's the way I want it, Mac." She tilted her head to one side. "You owe me my privacy. You owe me that."

"When will I see you again?"

"At the office next week. We have a meeting with Newt about the newsletter, remember?"

"Will you call me when you get home tonight?"

"No." She fought for words that would soften the sting. "I . . . couldn't talk to you . . . with any semblance of . . . dignity. It's better not to talk . . . at all." His head slumped. "Good-bye," she whispered. She opened the door and Mac jerked his gaze up to hers again.

"No." He kept his hands on her face until she reached up and slowly pulled away. "No. Not this way. Dear God, I never thought we'd come to this."

"Good-bye, Mac. This is the best way."

"Retta, I love you."

She used her last ounce of composure. "I love you, too. Good-bye."

"Good-bye," he managed finally. His hands were still

reaching for her as she stumbled out of the car and shut the door.

Why were minor duties such a physical and emotional strain these days? Retta bent over her rough draft of the ethics newsletter's first issue, forcing herself to concentrate on a story about the American Medical Association's new life-support rule.

There, she thought with a sigh. I'm reading. I'm concentrating. Here goes. "Can we ever morally justify the withholding of food from an irreversibly comatose patient?"

She recognized every word. Now if she only knew what she'd just read. Disgusted with her state of mind, she threw down the red pen with which she'd been making corrections and swiveled in her chair to look out the office window. The receptionist buzzed her intercom line.

"Dr. McHale is here. He's already in the conference room with Dr. Winston and Hilda. Scott and Vanessa just walked in, too."

"Thanks, Becky. I'll be right down."

Her hands shook violently as she gathered her rough draft and the pen. After four days of lonely hell, how could she be calm when she saw Mac again? Retta dug her fingernails into the newsletter's pages as she walked to the stairs. A sense of painful anticipation tore at her.

Mac stood up when she entered the conference room. It was an unnecessary gesture in the context of a business meeting—a gallant, yearning gesture of welcome that combined with the sadness in his expression and nearly overwhelmed her.

"Hello," she said, then sat down as gracefully as her trembling knees would let her.

"Hello." He never stopped looking at her as he settled back into his own chair. Everyone else in the room was innocently unaware that anything was wrong. Retta hadn't told Scott or Vanessa about Saturday's decision. She couldn't talk about it, could barely think about it, even now.

Newt clapped his hands together in delight, and grinned. "Well! Isn't it wonderful to know this is our last meeting? Next week we'll send the first issue of *Ethics in Health Care* to the printers." He leaned toward Mac. "I just want to thank you for all your personal attention. I assure you that an occasional phone call from us is all you need worry about after this. We hired an editor for the newsletter this week, and he'll be in touch."

"That's fine," Mac said tonelessly. Inside, he ached. Winston was cutting his last lifeline to Retta.

Newt chuckled in his usual high-pitched tone. "And in honor of this last meeting I want to make a couple of special announcements." Retta watched fixedly as her fingers guided her pen in endless circles on a corner of the newsletter's front page. She couldn't look into Mac's eyes anymore.

"First of all," Newt bubbled, "Ms. Isabella Edwards and I are engaged."

Retta raised her eyes to stare at him. He went on talking, chortling about their marriage plans, and she fought an odd, squeezing feeling inside her throat. She wanted to laugh, but the sound that twisted against her windpipe had too much bitter irony in it. She jerked her gaze back to the soothing, hypnotic scrawl of her pen. She could feel Mac's eyes burning into her.

"And I want to announce that Hilda is leaving us to go back to school full time." Being Hilda's assistant, Retta had already received this news. She glanced at Scott and Vanessa in time to see them struggling to hide their delighted shock behind neutral expressions. They were so comical that she almost smiled.

"I've always wanted to get my master's in literature," Hilda explained to everyone. She fiddled a strand of her lanky blond hair. "I want to do a thesis on German and Russian writers of the twentieth century."

"How fascinating," Scott said softly.

Retta almost failed to repress the smile this time. She could read Scott's thoughts: How fascinating, Hilda. You're going to study your idols. Stalin, Hitler . . .

Newt was saying something else, something about the editorial banana bunch being incomplete without a top banana. Here comes the rest of his announcement, Retta thought without happiness. She already knew this part, too.

" . . .so I'm sure it's no surprise to any of you that Retta is going to take over as executive editor." Scott clapped a hand on her back in enthusiastic congratulation, and Vanessa applauded. Retta looked at each of them and nodded her thanks. "Retta knows how difficult and demanding the job can be," Newt continued. "It requires almost complete dedication. And I know I can depend on Retta to give that dedication."

Mac watched her through narrowed, disbelieving eyes. She didn't want that damned job. She'd told him on more than one occasion that it had worn Hilda down over the years, that it meant long, brutal hours—more nights, more weekends, more holidays. The salary increase would be enormous, but it wasn't worth it. Why had she accepted?

Retta didn't look at him. She knew he disapproved. It didn't matter, because she needed the extra work to keep her sane. She didn't know anything else to do for her grief but to work it out of her soul. She'd leave only the sparest amount of time for missing him, and that way she'd be able to cope.

"Congratulations," he said tautly. Retta looked up at him then, her eyes damp with tears. He reached inside his sports coat and, without the least bit of hocus-pocus, retrieved a rosebud. Her throat closed with sadness. She'd grown to expect these whimsical flowers from him. But now . . .

"What, no more magic?" she asked, forcing herself to smile. No more? she asked again, silently. Oh, Mac. Retta held her hand out and he placed the tiny red bud in her palm. He shook his head slowly, his eyes empty and tired.

"I've lost my touch," he answered gruffly.

Retta was amazed at all the efficient and orderly chores she accomplished in the short periods of time sandwiched between waking and sleeping and working. Over the next week she sewed two new skirts, scrubbed the inside of her refrigerator, wallpapered her bathroom, cleaned the crevices in her old stovetop with cotton swabs, and had time left over to reread *Gone with the Wind*.

This time she cried not just when Rhett left Scarlett at the end of the book, but every time he left her throughout the course of the book, and even when he just talked about leaving. After that, Retta resolved to confine her pleasure reading to medical journals.

She was utterly depressed Friday afternoon at work when she realized that an absolutely immaculate apartment waited for her at home and that her office desk had not one urgent memo or "must read" file folder left on it.

She'd worked herself into a corner with nothing to do but think about Mac. No. She'd play golf, something she hadn't done since the Saturday when Mac had to perform the emergency operation. The Saturday when she'd told him good-bye. That was almost two weeks ago.

She was on the municipal course by five o'clock, her face raised toward the August sun, her old clubs hanging heavy on her shoulder. She'd replaced the broken driver with a new one from the clubs Mac had bought for her. By the time she reached the ninth tee, she'd begun to wonder if she shouldn't break the rest of her clubs and give golf up for good. Slice, hook, slice, hook.

She teed up, stood back, and swung ferociously. The golf ball made a long, powerful arch into dense oak forest on her right. Retta's shoulders slumped. She leaned heavily on her driver, as if it were a cane. Was it possible that she'd never hit a golf ball straight down the fairway again? Was it possible that Mac had taken even this magic out of her life?

"Fore!" a deep voice yelled.

Startled, she clutched her driver to her chest and covered her head with one arm just before she heard the soft thud of a golf ball landing in the sod behind her. Her thinly drawn patience snapped like brittle glass.

"Why are you hitting so close to the tee?" she yelled

back. She uncovered her head and looked over her shoulder toward the eighth green. "It makes no sense . . ."

Of course it didn't. It was Mac.

She turned around and stood frozen in place, her pulse thumping in her ears as she watched him stride down the fairway toward her. His handsome leather golf bag swung easily from one big shoulder, and he held one of his clubs tilted over the other shoulder at a jaunty angle.

"Good afternoon," he said politely, when he reached the tee. "Mind if I play through?"

He looked down at her with a teasing smile, but the old starved expression in his eyes told her all the humor was a facade. Retta took a step back while her greedy senses absorbed everything about him.

The golden brown hair, now a little grayer around the temples than it had been two weeks ago, the thin look of his dear face, his athletic body a little too angular in his white shorts and blue sports shirt. The man wasn't eating right. But then, neither was she.

"What happened?" she asked with just as much false humor. "Did someone discover oil in the country club course? Is it closed for drilling? Why are you here?"

"I just wanted to try something different. You talked about this course so much that I thought I'd come here today." Today, yesterday, the day before—every afternoon for the past week he'd come here, looking for her. But he didn't tell her that.

"Uh huh," she said skeptically. "Well, I have to go find my golf ball, in the rough over there. Good-bye."

"It looks rough, even for rough," he quipped, squinting at the giant oak trees and thick shrubbery. "You'd better just take a penalty and start over with a new golf ball."

"Golf balls cost money." She slung her bag over her back and started down the hill toward the woods. He caught up with her quickly.

"Well, you got a huge raise, didn't you? You might as well enjoy that part of your new position."

"I like being austere, Mac. It's my nature."

Why the hell had he come here today to torment her?

What did he want? Every impulse in her cried out to drop this nonchalant front and ask him what this visit meant. She walked faster.

They entered the cool, shadowy woodland without speaking. Her bag caught on a low limb and she set it down. Mac set his beside it. Goose bumps ran up Retta's arms and she forced her gaze to remain on the ground, searching . . . for something . . . oh yes, the golf ball. She felt Mac's presence in a sensual way that was undeniably pleasant and primal. These woods hid them from the view of other golfers.

"Look for the ball over there," she said briskly, and pointed. "I'll look over here."

"I'd better stay near you. There might be wild animals in these woods," he informed her. "Feral dogs. Rabid raccoons. Snakes. A Bigfoot."

"A big fake." She looked up at him with wretched eyes. "Why are you really here, Mac? Why?"

His teasing attitude faded instantly, and he shook his head in grim self-rebuke. "Because I'm miserable without you, and this is the only excuse I have to see you."

"It's not fair." Her voice trembled. "All I want is for you to leave me alone."

"That's not true," he said hoarsely. "You don't want to be left alone."

She looked at him for a long, tragic moment. "All right, so I'm not worth a damn without you. What do you want me to do?" Her voice rose with the strain of not crying. "Love you? Not love you?"

"Love me."

"But not permanently," she murmured. She swallowed hard and covered her face with both hands.

"Love me," he repeated in a broken voice. He stepped forward and took her in his arms. Retta cried out in bitter resistance to his familiar warmth, his hard, masculine body, the tender caress of his lips against her forehead. "Love me," he nearly begged. "Come back to me."

Then his mouth was on hers, cajoling sensually, wanton and hungry. She pressed her fists into his shoulders, dug her fingers into the soft material of his shirt and the hard muscle beneath. The physical need in her was no more potent than the ache of neglected emotions. The combination was overwhelming.

"Mac," she groaned in defeat. She conformed her body to his in a rough, demanding way that seethed with frustration as well as desire. She buried her face in his neck and inhaled the clean, hot scent of his skin. "Take me," she whispered. "Make love to me just one more time."

His hands were roving up and down her arched back. Now they stopped, holding her in a fierce grip. Not just one more time, he told her silently. Think that if you want to, but it's not the last time. It can't be.

"You'll stay with me tonight, if I do," he said swiftly. "You'll come home with me. You'll talk to me."

"All right," she moaned. "One night."

"One night," he echoed. Then he lowered her to the soft, matted leaves beneath a gracious old oak. She jerked at his clothes in haste, tormented by the need to feel his nakedness next to her, to believe that he was real. He was no less anxious for her, and he pulled her tailored shorts and neatly ironed top away from her body with fierce tugs of his hands.

"You're wearing these prim old things again," he told her between short breaths. "I won't have it. I won't have you trying to look plain and ordinary. I want you naked."

And soon he had her that way, writhing under him as he fervently worshiped every part of her with his hands and mouth. She bit her lip and struggled to push away from him when the pleasure became so intense she thought she'd cry out. But he followed her with his caresses and words of such intense devotion that he seemed to be in touch with some deep spring of spiritual inspiration.

"I dream about you at night," he rasped against her neck, as their bodies joined. "Retta, my sweet little Retta. You're all I need. Where's my magic gone? You took it. You took it with you . . ."

"No. Gone. I don't . . . have it either." She arched wildly against him, caught in so many sensations that she couldn't absorb them all. The gracious old trees filled her vision overhead; their discarded leaves scratched deliciously underneath her. Mac's wonderful voice and generous hands and deep, thrusting movements entranced her.

She inhaled deeply, then let the overload of sensation flow out of her for several long, shuddering moments. Before she breathed again Mac joined her in the release, his mouth on hers, his groan of pleasure tickling her lips, his hands on either side of her face as if he were focusing all his love into her glowing eyes.

Their breathing quieted while he kissed her slowly and possessively. When he began to ease himself away she stopped him.

"Not yet," she whispered.

He nodded, then arranged his big body on her as carefully as he could. She trailed her toes down the backs of his legs.

"Ouch," he said suddenly. Retta gasped. She realized then that she still wore her short white socks and golf shoes, with their sharp metal cleats. And he still wore his. "I bet we've dug some interesting trenches during this . . . encounter," he teased breathlessly. "Somebody will think two giant gophers have been here."

It was too embarrassing, too funny, too outrageous for her to imagine what they must have looked like making passionate love in the midst of the woods, wearing nothing but those goofy-looking shoes.

Retta began to giggle, her head thrown back and her cheek pressed against Mac's jaw. He chuckled, and the vibrations went all the way through her. She held him tightly.

"Amadeus," she murmured in an airy voice. "Only with you, Amadeus. You're the only man who could possibly have gotten me to do something this insane in broad daylight."

His arms slid under her in a possessive embrace. "You ain't seen nothing yet," he promised.

CHAPTER TWELVE

BECAUSE THEY NEEDED each other so much, it was possible to momentarily submerge their problems in the sheer joy of being together again, Retta admitted that night. It was possible to laugh, to hug, to share a quiet dinner and then just lie together and talk on Mac's living room couch, ignoring the future.

They went to bed very early—and very naked. But she simply snuggled close beside him under the intimate light of his bedside lamp while he read to her from one of Edgar Rice Burroughs's *Tarzan* books.

"You do a great Johnny Weissmuller," she commented with drowsy appreciation. "But your Maureen O'Sullivan is too baritone."

"How about my monkey sound effects?"

"Perfect. You were born to the part."

"I say, you rude hyena!" he exclaimed in an absurd British accent. "I shall have to chastise you for your complete lack of manners."

He tossed the book down and began to tickle her. Retta squealed and kicked and tickled back until they were both breathless and the bedspread lay on the floor.

"Ape! Gorilla!" she taunted, as he tried to bite her leg. She slapped his lean rump with the flat of her hand. "Shoo!"

"Want to touch my banana?"

166

"N-no!" she sputtered, laughing. She stretched out on her back and Mac cradled her shoulders in the crook of his arm. He arranged himself on his side, then slipped his other arm under her knees. He pulled her legs up and draped them over his top thigh, then drew his knees against her bottom.

"Now I've got you," he murmured.

They shared a loving gaze. "Uh-huh," she answered softly. She tilted her face up so that their mouths could meet for a light, lingering kiss. In the midst of it, the bed-side telephone buzzed.

"Ooooh, you make me hear electronic sounds," he quipped.

"Thank you, but that one's not my doing."

He tweaked her breast and rolled over. She rolled over, too, and nestled against his strong, well-formed back, nuzzling a patch of hair midway between his shoulder blades.

"I hope you don't have to go to the hospital," she said forlornly.

"Me, too." He answered the phone and she listened as he murmured calm replies to someone's words. "Yes. Where? Yes. I'll be right there." He put the phone back in its receiver and lay very still for a second.

"Phooey," she said with more cheerfulness than she felt. "Mac, you better hurry back . . ."

"It's Lucas." He sat up and swung his feet off the side of the bed, then jammed both hands into his hair.

Retta felt the blood drain out of her face. She leaped up beside him and saw his stricken, drawn expression. "Oh, honey. What?"

Mac stared at the floor. "He was . . . playing football with friends. He was tackled . . . hard . . . hit in the head."

"Mac," she said in dread.

His stunned gaze rose to hers. It was full of quiet despair. "He's unconscious." Action suddenly snapped into him. He lurched off the bed and ran to the closet.

"I'm going with you," she said quickly, and ran to get her shorts and top. On her way past him he reached out and grabbed her hand. His eyes were tortured.

"I want you to drive. I don't trust my coordination right now."

She hugged him tightly. "Everything will be fine," she whispered into his ear. And then, just because he needed to hear it, "I love you."

As she went to dress, she prayed silently that Lucas wouldn't die.

Subdural hematoma. Retta shivered at the words and thought that even Mac's quiet, soothing voice hadn't made them sound less horrible than they were. She hugged herself and pulled Mac's light windbreaker tighter over her thin golf blouse.

With her bare legs curled under her she felt anchored to the sticky vinyl of the waiting room's couch. A voice on the old television set in one corner welcomed Chicago's WGN Channel 9 viewers to the late-night movie.

Late night? she thought ruefully, her body leaden with exhaustion. Retta glanced at her wrist watch. Three A.M. It wasn't late night, it was early morning. But time was a meaningless concept here, anyway. She felt as if several lifetimes had passed since Mac went into the operating room to watch a neurosurgeon repair the damage done by a ruptured blood vessel in the outermost lining of Lucas's brain. But it had only been two hours.

The sound of footsteps outside the waiting room made her jump. Retta looked up quickly as Mac walked in, his face creased with strain and his hair ruffled. He still wore the light blue pants and footings of his surgical outfit. His white undershirt was damp with perspiration. Retta stood up.

"How is he, Mac?" He stopped in front of her and ran one hand over his face. He swayed—very slightly—and she grabbed his arm. "Sit down, Amadeus."

He nodded and sank onto the couch, then slid an arm around her shoulders as she sat down next to him. Mac leaned his forehead against hers. "I don't know," he said softly. "The procedure was beautiful. He ought to be fine. I don't know."

"He's in recovery?"

"Yes. As soon as they move him into intensive care I'll go back."

"Can I go with you?"

His hand took hers in a pressing grip, as if he wanted to draw from her strength. "Thanks. Yes."

They sat still, just holding each other. Finally she stroked the back of his head. "Mac, I told Lucas's friends to go downstairs and get some fresh air. I felt so bad for them. They're taking this hard. I think the fact that it was such a freak accident makes it worse."

"Sometimes it doesn't take a hard blow to cause this kind of injury." Mac sighed. "He'll recover without any problem." There was a deadly pause. "If...he... recovers..."

"Hush!" She leaned back and gazed at him sternly, but let her voice tease him a little. "Dr. Kildare would never talk that way. He was my idol, until I met you, so don't tamper with my fantasy."

A tiny smile crooked one corner of Mac's mouth. He leaned back on the couch and rested his head against the pale green wall behind it. His eyes closed. "Don't die, Luke," he whispered.

Retta had the uncanny feeling that she was looking inside him, seeing the deep, unresolved bitterness and grief that Judith's death had left behind. Sorrow filled her and she touched his face lightly, caressing, soothing. His eyes remained shut.

"Tell me about him, Amadeus. Tell me everything you can remember about him when he was little. Every detail."

"Why?" His voice held defeat.

"Because it will help you to think about him the way he was then, not the way he is now."

His eyes opened slowly, full of wonder and memories. He squinted at her in tired, teasing suspicion. "Where did you get so much wisdom, Henrietta?"

"From loving and being loved by a lot of terrific people."

He nodded, smiling in a way that made her feel very

loved by him, in particular. With renewed strength in his voice, he began to talk about his son.

How could Lucas look so healthy and still remain unconscious? Seated beside his bed in a straight-backed chair, Retta studied his handsome, peaceful face and thought how all the white around him made his skin seem even more tanned and warm.

His head was swathed in a skullcap of white gauze and tape. Tubes and wires radiated from him like a spider web. Twenty-four hours. It seemed impossible that he had lain there for twenty-four hours since the surgery without moving. She leaned forward, her eyes riveted to him.

Fight this, she begged silently. Wake up. Your father loves you so much. I love you because you're part of him. Please.

Suddenly Mac's fingertips touched her cheek. He brushed her hair back behind her ear with a gentle motion. "Are you talking to Luke again?" he asked in a low, gruff voice.

"Yes." Mac's fingers touched her cheek a second time and she turned to place a kiss on them. "It's working. I can feel him listening, Mac."

"I know," he murmured. "Keep it up."

A short, robust man in rumpled brown corduroy stepped inside the open door of the tiny intensive-care room. He pushed thick glasses up on his nose with one hand and reached out with the other as Mac rose to his feet. They shook hands warmly. The visitor winked at Retta, and she smiled. Marshall Hicks, Lucas's surgeon, reminded her of a teddy bear.

"His vitals are good, Marshall," Mac said earnestly, as if he was trying to reassure himself that everything was fine. "He just needs a little more time."

"I know, I know." Marshall patted Mac's shoulder. "But Mac, we need to talk about what we're going to do if he stays this way."

"He isn't classified 'coma,'" Mac replied, sounding almost defensive. "You can't—"

"I know, buddy, I know." Marshall's voice was soothing and deliberately jovial. "But we're going to have to feed the boy, Mac. I'm going to order a nasogastric tube."

Retta watched in anxiety as Mac's hands clenched into fists. She got up hurriedly and went to him, taking one of her hands in his. He clasped his fingers around hers with a fierce grip.

"Okay," he told Marshall in a voice strained with control, "if . . . his condition deteriorates I want him to have everything he needs to keep going. The feeding tube, the respirator, full life support. As long as he needs it."

"All right, all right," Marshall said gently, patting his hands at Mac in a calming gesture. "McHale, he'd have to go downhill a lot before we'd need to discuss all this. Relax."

"No, I can't relax," Mac answered. Retta heard the misery in his tone, and she squeezed his hand in sympathy. "I want everyone on staff to understand. There'll be no DNR orders given."

"No 'do not resuscitate'?" Marshall blinked in shock. "Mac, that's not even a concern at this point. The boy's not even in a coma!"

"Amadeus, you're giving Marshall high blood pressure," Retta teased very carefully. "Calm down."

"I'm not here to ask for organ donations, Mac, for Pete's sake," Marshall added, perturbed.

Mac's eyes narrowed in pain. "I'll make that decision at the last minute, dammit! I won't talk about it now."

"Nobody asked you to talk about it, for crying out loud."

Retta shook her head at Marshall, signaling him to give up. "Order the nasogastric tube," she instructed. "We'll sit back down and wait."

Mac's shoulders slumped. "Marshall, I'm sorry for being like this," he began.

"Aw, forget it." Marshall slapped his arm. "You cardiology boys are high strung. I expect it."

He left, smiling grimly, and Mac sighed in deep exhaustion. Retta tugged at his hand.

"Come on, Amadeus," she murmured. "Sit down and behave."

When they were seated again he leaned forward and rested his elbows on his knees. He gave Lucas a long, desperate look and then bowed his head. Retta put a hand on the middle of his back and rubbed tranquil circles.

"I won't let him go," Mac whispered. "As long as there's any chance, I won't let him go. And when there's not . . . I'll say good-bye. The rules are different now. He won't linger the way Judith did. I worked hard to make certain the damned rules would be different."

He looked at her in despair, and his voice dropped. "But none of that will bring him back. I wish I could see the future."

Retta shook her head, and tears slid down her cheeks. "Mac, all any of us have is this day, this moment. The future isn't important. There are no guarantees for anybody." She paused. "No guarantees except love. You won't stop loving Lucas, no matter what happens. I won't stop loving you. I hope you won't stop loving me."

"I won't," he answered hoarsely.

"Touchdown," Lucas mumbled.

Mac jumped up and Retta followed breathlessly. They bent over Lucas and watched his eyelids flicker. Mac slowly touched his son's cheek.

"Luke," he said in a shivering, low voice. Lucas's blue eyes blinked open and met Mac's weakly. But the corner of his mouth managed to inch upward in a hint of humor.

"I guess . . . I didn't score," he mumbled. "Feel like somebody tackled the hell . . . out of me."

"Somebody did," Mac answered. Retta watched a huge grin spread across Mac's face. "But you're a champ, anyway."

Retta was surprised when Lucas's eyes moved to her. "Hi there," she said gently, and patted his arm. "We missed you."

His smile grew a fraction of an inch stronger. "Henrietta. Glad you're . . . with Dad." He paused. "Hard head, he's got. Like . . . mine."

"Thank goodness," she answered, and knew she was grinning as widely as Mac. "It saved your life."

A nurse bustled into the room, followed by Marshall. "Well, well," the little neurosurgeon chortled. "Mr. McHale's vital signs just took a leap. What have we here?"

"Hungry," Lucas told everyone in a faint voice.

"Good. Eating's part of the prescribed treatment," Marshall answered cheerfully. "I guess you can do it the old-fashioned way now. Without a tube."

Through all this Mac had simply stood mesmerized, his eyes gleaming with relief and happiness as he gazed at Lucas.

Retta looked away and brushed the dampness from her eyes. Lucas was going to be all right, thank God. But this experience could only have convinced Mac that permanent relationships were full of too much risk and pain.

"Well, we always said that slaves can't be fired, they have to be sold," Scott quipped grimly. Retta propped her chin on her hand and leaned morosely on her office desk. Her expression somber, she looked at Scott and Vanessa, seated across from her. Vanessa raised a soft-drink can in a whimsical salute.

"Here's to National Health being part of a conglomerate."

"Medical Franchise Publishing isn't a conglomerate, it's a universe," Scott corrected. "And we're the smallest planet in the smallest solar system on the edge of that universe. We're space dust."

"I didn't want to be executive editor anyhow," Retta murmured. "I might get used to having money in my savings account. It could be addictive. I'd sit around at the end of every quarter, waiting for my interest statement, my eyes glazed..."

"What are you going to do?" Vanessa asked. "Swallow your pride and go back to being assistant executive editor when Medical Franchise sends in the new management team?"

"No." Retta shook her head. "I've swallowed so much

pride over the years that I feel like a balloon. I'm going to find another job."

"Me, too," Scott said tautly. Vanessa looked at them both for a second.

"Me, too," she chimed in firmly.

"All for one and one for all!" Scott stood and lifted his hand as if he held a sword pointed toward heaven.

"Bravo!" Vanessa chorused and imitated his gesture.

"The Three Mouseketeers!" Retta exclaimed. She stood and saluted them. Mac's insanity has captured me, she thought briefly. Before I met him, I'd never have been this giddy and impulsive.

"That's Musketeers," Scott corrected drolly. She gave him a grand look of derision.

"You live in your fantasy, Scott, and I'll live in mine." Her office phone buzzed. "Yes, Becky?"

"Dr. Ama-Amadoogus McHale on line two."

"We shall scram," Vanessa said primly. She and Scott dropped their imaginary swords and left the office. Smiling, Retta tapped a button on her phone and picked up the receiver.

"Amadoogus, how was your visit with Lucas today?"

"Amadoogus?" he asked.

"Becky got your name wrong. Sorry."

"That's all right, I like it." He chuckled. "Luke is terrific. He was moved out of intensive care today. The nurses are fighting over who gets to give him his daily sponge bath. He's very happy. How are you, my sweet young thing?"

Her smile wavered. "I'm job hunting."

"What?" Immediately, the humor left his voice. "Honey, what happened?"

She told him that Newt had just informed the department heads that he was selling the company to Medical Franchise Publishing, in Los Angeles.

"Mac, listen to this." She couldn't help chuckling, although she buried her face in one hand as she did. "He said, 'We're going to mix our ingredients with theirs.' I felt like a jar of oregano."

"Honey," he said soothingly, "it's for the best. You should get out of that place and do what you really want to do. Write children's books."

"Oh, Mac, that's just a silly little notion . . ."

"No, it's not. Not if you really want to do it."

"Well, that's beside the point. I'm going to find another job . . ."

"Not tonight, you're not. You're going to bring your quaint little fanny over to my place and let me coddle and adore you."

She smiled sadly, glad that he couldn't see her face. Her job at National Health had been the mainstay of her lonely life before he came into it. Now there was every possibility that she wouldn't have her job or Mac. Nothing was settled between the two of them. They were ignoring the future, marking time under the pretense that they were going to share it.

"I could really enjoy being coddled and adored tonight," she said hoarsely. She was greedy to get every moment she could with him. "Thank you."

They sat at a wicker table in the garden room, quietly watching night settle over Lake Michigan. The tall candles Mac had placed in the table's center seemed to flicker in sync with the blinking ship lights on the distant horizon, and magenta streaks slipped from the sky into the water, joining the two together like lovers, Retta thought.

Mac gathered their dishes and stood up. "Wait right here, and I'll bring dessert."

"Wow. This is great coddling and adoring," she mused.

"I'm honing my skills."

Why? she wondered dully. Will we be together much longer?

In a few minutes he came back carrying a bottle of champagne in an ice bucket, and two tall, fluted glasses. She smiled in wonder. "Amadeus, this elevates coddling and adoring to a much higher level."

He bent forward and touched his mouth to hers for a

long, gentle kiss. When he drew back she still had her eyes closed. He kissed each lid. "Mmmmm," she responded.

"I'm sorry about your job," he whispered. "I'll make it up to you."

She opened her eyes and gazed at him wistfully. "Thank you for caring, Mac . . ."

"With magic," he interjected. "Just give me a minute to get organized."

Surprised at this turn of events, she watched as he set the champagne glasses in front of her. He tossed a cloth napkin over the bottle and began twisting the cork.

"*Sacré bleu!*" he muttered in terrible French, like a befuddled wine steward in an elegant restaurant. "Zee bottle, she eez treees deeficult, like ma woman eez deeficult, always wanteeng to wrestle . . ." Retta began to giggle, and covered her mouth with one hand. He was so dear.

A loud pop signaled his victory. "There she poofs!" Mac said in the same awful accent as before. Grinning, he poured champagne into both glasses and set the bottle in its bucket.

"How pretty!" she said in a soft voice. "Look at the way the candlelight reflects through the champagne, Mac." Retta reached for her glass.

"Wait!" he said without an accent. "I have to do the floor show."

She withdrew her hand and gave him a wry look. "I'm glad you got your magic touch back . . . I think." She studied him admiringly. "Is this why you look so terrific? For your performance?" He wore a dress shirt, a beautiful gray tie, and smoky gray trousers.

"Of course. Now watch carefully." He stood beside the table about an arm's length from her, his back straight and his chin up. Using the same napkin as before, he covered his hand. "Say the magic words."

"Mickey Mouse," she offered.

"*Voilá!*" He whipped the napkin away and held out a colorful bouquet of magician's paper flowers. "For you!"

She took them and knew she must look like a delighted kid who'd just been kissed for the first time. "How fantastic!" she gushed. Retta peered at his innocent-looking shirt sleeves. She'd never figure out where he hid things.

"And now . . . my God, Retta, look at you!"

Startled, she looked down at her pleated yellow blouse and slender white skirt. She put her bouquet onto the table. "What?"

"You're sprouting roses!"

"Oh, you're teasing . . ." she began, but his hands stopped her with their sudden, delicious assault. They roamed quickly, darting behind her ears, between her knees, under her chin. They trailed across her breasts with wicked skill.

And with every movement, rosebuds fell in her lap.

"Mac!" she exclaimed in disbelief. He must have had two dozen of the delicate little buds in his possession. He tucked one behind both of her ears, eased one into the buttonhole between her breasts, worked several into her hair. "Oh, Amadeus! Oh, this is wonderful!"

She gathered the rest of the ruby-red blossoms out of her lap and cupped the sweet scent to her face. "I'll never forget this," she murmured brokenly. "Never."

Mac stepped back, his chest moving fast with erratic, short breaths. "Just wait," he told her.

She gazed at him in speechless expectation as he took the napkin into his hands again. "Now watch the champagne glass on your right," he instructed softly. "It's going to change."

She tilted her head to one side and watched with a tiny, incredulous smile as he dropped the napkin in front of the glasses. He held it there like a curtain, dangling tautly from his fingertips. "Say the magic words," he ordered again.

"I love you," she whispered, and raised a teary gaze to his face. He looked at her tenderly. His voice came out very deep and soft.

"That ought to do it." He smiled at her. "Now watch the champagne glass."

She turned obedient eyes back to the napkin. "Voilá," he murmured, and lifted it.

And there, glinting in the bottom of one glass, shimmering in gold and light, was a simple, magnificent diamond in a Tiffany setting.

"I know," he whispered. "It's an odd way to offer you an engagement ring."

"It's . . . it's a what?"

He knelt beside her and slid both arms around her waist. Retta turned her stunned gaze from the glittering ring submerged in champagne to his face. His eyes were somber.

"An engagement ring. If you're still interested in having me for a husband."

She struggled to make sense of his change in attitude. She put both hands on his shoulders. Test, yes. He felt real, very strong and secure. This was no dream.

"Are you interested in having a wife?" she asked with an incredulous tone.

"Not just any wife. You."

"But . . . risks . . . children . . ."

"Some people live in the past. I've been living in the future, always arranging my life to avoid being hurt again. Maybe the incident with Lucas reaffirmed my faith in the future, because he didn't die. I don't know. But I've been thinking ever since—if he had died, I'd still have fantastic memories from all the years we shared. I have those memories of Judith, I just forgot how to appreciate them."

Mac paused, then inhaled deeply. "Who have I been kidding? I can no more give you up than I could give up Lucas. I'll hold on to you, fight for you, love you, no matter what." His hands rose to her face. "Let's make some memories, Retta. Marry me."

"This is very sudden, and not very logical," she whispered in a barely audible voice. He nodded. She smiled. "That's why I like it." Her voice rose merrily. "Of course I'll marry you, Amadeus! Haven't I loved you since the day we met?"

"Illogical, illogical," he rebuked as he pulled her to him for an ecstatic kiss. "Mmmmm." Another kiss. "Impractical." A third kiss, and she was off the chair, kneeling on the floor with him, holding him tightly. "But quaint. I like quaint."

"The champagne," she murmured, already tipsy from excitement. They reached for the glasses, then intertwined their arms so that she could drink from his glass and he could drink from hers. The crystal made a delicate sound when they tipped the glasses together.

"I love you, Henrietta Pauline," he said gently.

"And I love you, Bronson Amadeus."

She sipped from his glass, then watched, wide-eyed, as Mac emptied hers in one long swallow. He deftly caught the ring between his lips. When he looked down at her left hand expectantly, she raised it to his mouth.

She placed her third finger through the ring and he nudged it into place, kissing her hand throughout the process. They both looked at the elegant, gleaming diamond for a moment. Then their eyes met.

"It's magic," she told him.

He smiled. No. The magic was in her eyes.

EPILOGUE

SHE WAS WARM, and the pillow felt incredibly soft beneath her head. The smooth comforter caressed her shoulder. But something was wrong.

Retta blinked awake in the dark as if some sixth sense had gone on alert. Then she realized why—Mac was no longer asleep beside her. She sat up and gazed groggily around the big bedroom, running her hands through hair that had grown long enough to curl halfway down her shoulder blades.

She covered her flannel nightgown with a long robe and walked out of the room into a dimly lit hall, where she stopped to listen. Then she smiled. He was down in the den, watching television. In the condo she would have heard every bit of the program, but sound didn't travel as well in their big suburban home.

Retta walked past the open door of a partially decorated nursery, then stopped at her office. She peeked at her desk to make certain she'd turned the word processor off for the night.

Writing free-lance medical articles and struggling to break into children's fiction at the same time was no easy task, and the clutter of her office showed that. The word processor was still humming, and she shook her head in self-rebuke as she remedied the oversight. Even at three months, pregnancy had a distracting effect on her concentration.

Retta patted the slight bulge around her navel affectionately and continued downstairs. When she reached the den she came to an abrupt stop, gazing in amused disbelief at what she saw.

So the man was sneaking out of bed to watch tapes of *Sesame Street*.

He leaned back in a cozy leather recliner, his bare feet crossed on the footrest, his robe tucked around him, a book lying unopened in his lap. He had his chin propped on one hand and he seemed to be enthralled by something Big Bird was saying to Oscar.

"Amadeus, you're the most dedicated father-to-be I've ever seen," she said in gentle reproach. "You need to get some sleep."

When he swiveled his head toward her she caught the sheepish expression on his face. Then he smiled, and tapped a button on the television's remote control. Big Bird and Oscar disappeared into a blank screen.

"Come here and set your growing body on my lap," he teased. "Before you get too huge for me to accommodate."

"You promised that you'd be nice to me when I'm a blimp," she reminded him as she walked toward the recliner. Smiling, Retta stopped beside it and he reached for her hand.

"I will. But in self-defense, I may not let you sit on my lap." He pushed his book aside and gently pulled her into the chair with him. "I'll just have to get all my lap-snuggling in early." Mac kissed her forehead and she nestled deep into his arms. Retta chuckled as she glanced at the title of the book. The well-known author's name made her laugh.

"You always call me Mr. Spock. Can I call you Dr. Spock?" she asked coyly.

"No, you feisty mama. You may not."

"After raising Lucas, you don't need any textbook guidance on how to be a good father. Lucas is a fine example of good parenting."

"That, lovely lady, was many years ago. I intend to perfect my methods. If we're going to have three or four children . . ."

"Three or four? What happened to the two we discussed right after we got married?"

"Well," he said, nodding for emphasis, "the idea sort of grew on me."

"Good heavens! Four little McHales running amok with all their father's energy?"

"They'll keep you young," he protested.

She kissed him boisterously. "You, Amadeus, keep me young. But I'll consider your suggestion."

"You're only as old as you feel," he told her. "That's my clichéd old theory." He winked devilishly at her.

Retta felt a languid, familiar heat inside her body as he opened her robe and molded her nightgown to her breasts with the gentle exploration of his hands.

"Hmmm. Let me check something, Mac." She drew his robe open and did some exploring of her own. His stomach tightened as her hand trailed down the bare skin and untied his pajama bottoms.

"Oh, how wonderful, how handsome," she whispered as her exploration continued. He shifted in the chair, and Retta looked up to find his blue eyes gleaming with desire.

"Amadeus, if you're only as old as you feel . . ."—she smiled tenderly as he kissed her—"then I'd say you're about . . . oh, twenty-one, twenty-two. Not a day older."

"Do you want me to prove my theory?" he murmured. "It may take a long time. How many years do you have?"

She looked at him with adoring eyes. Her answer was timeless.

SECOND CHANCE AT LOVE

COMING NEXT MONTH

STRANGER FROM THE PAST #422
by Jan Mathews

Destiny reunites Reanna Williamson
with the darkly handsome stranger who
fathered her child five years earlier.
Now wealthy racehorse breeder
Travis Martin treats Reanna like a
headstrong filly ripe for his mastery—
and she's prepared to give him the
challenge of his life!

HEAVEN SENT #423
by Jamisan Whitney

When their bikes collide,
Bree Jeffries and Sam Leong become
entwined…and he's in no hurry to
untangle his long limbs from her curves.
But their bicycle messenger services
are in competition, and Bree's convinced
that Sam's "unsafe at any speed"—
until he teaches her the joys of
love in tandem…

Second Chance At Love

Be Sure to Read These New Releases!

CUPID'S CAMPAIGN #418
by Kate Gilbert
With zany humor and high-voltage
energy, this tale of dashing prosecutor
Frank Wade's infatuation with animal rights
crusader Allie Tarkington unfolds.
Thrown intimately together, they stalk
dognappers...and each other!

GAMBLER'S LADY #419
by Cait Logan
Masterful casino owner Nick Santos
plays poker with spunky Kim Reynolds for
high stakes—a marriage of convenience
against a monetary offer she can't refuse.
When Kim loses, she finds the forfeit
more disturbing—and tantalizing—
than she'd anticipated...

Order on opposite page

SECOND CHANCE AT LOVE

___ 0-425-09745-5	CUPID'S VERDICT #386 Jackie Leigh	$2.25
___ 0-425-09746-3	CHANGE OF HEART #387 Helen Carter	$2.25
___ 0-425-09831-1	PLACES IN THE HEART #388 Delaney Devers	$2.25
___ 0-425-09832-X	A DASH OF SPICE #389 Kerry Price	$2.25
___ 0-425-09833-8	TENDER LOVING CARE #390 Jeanne Grant	$2.25
___ 0-425-09834-6	MOONSHINE AND MADNESS #391 Kate Gilbert	$2.25
___ 0-425-09835-4	MADE FOR EACH OTHER #392 Aimee Duvall	$2.25
___ 0-425-09836-2	COUNTRY DREAMING #393 Samantha Quinn	$2.25
___ 0-425-09943-1	NO HOLDS BARRED #394 Jackie Leigh	$2.25
___ 0-425-09944-X	DEVIN'S PROMISE #395 Kelly Adams	$2.25
___ 0-425-09945-8	FOR LOVE OF CHRISTY #396 Jasmine Craig	$2.25
___ 0-425-09946-6	WHISTLING DIXIE #397 Adrienne Edwards	$2.25
___ 0-425-09947-4	BEST INTENTIONS #398 Sherryl Woods	$2.25
___ 0-425-09948-2	NIGHT MOVES #399 Jean Kent	$2.25
___ 0-425-10048-0	IN NAME ONLY #400 Mary Modean	$2.25
___ 0-425-10049-9	RECLAIM THE DREAM #401 Liz Grady	$2.25
___ 0-425-10050-2	CAROLINA MOON #402 Joan Darling	$2.25
___ 0-425-10051-0	THE WEDDING BELLE #403 Diana Morgan	$2.25
___ 0-425-10052-9	COURTING TROUBLE #404 Laine Allen	$2.25
___ 0-425-10053-7	EVERYBODY'S HERO #405 Jan Mathews	$2.25
___ 0-425-10080-4	CONSPIRACY OF HEARTS #406 Pat Dalton	$2.25
___ 0-425-10081-2	HEAT WAVE #407 Lee Williams	$2.25
___ 0-425-10082-0	TEMPORARY ANGEL #408 Courtney Ryan	$2.25
___ 0-425-10083-9	HERO AT LARGE #409 Steffie Hall	$2.25
___ 0-425-10084-7	CHASING RAINBOWS #410 Carole Buck	$2.25
___ 0-425-10085-5	PRIMITIVE GLORY #411 Cass McAndrew	$2.25
___ 0-425-10225-4	TWO'S COMPANY #412 Sherryl Woods	$2.25
___ 0-425-10226-2	WINTER FLAME #413 Kelly Adams	$2.25
___ 0-425-10227-0	A SWEET TALKIN' MAN #414 Jackie Leigh	$2.25
___ 0-425-10228-9	TOUCH OF MIDNIGHT #415 Kerry Price	$2.25
___ 0-425-10229-7	HART'S DESIRE #416 Linda Raye	$2.25
___ 0-425-10230-0	A FAMILY AFFAIR #417 Cindy Victor	$2.25
___ 0-425-10513-X	CUPID'S CAMPAIGN #418 Kate Gilbert	$2.50
___ 0-425-10514-8	GAMBLER'S LADY #419 Cait Logan	$2.50
___ 0-425-10515-6	ACCENT ON DESIRE #420 Christa Merlin	$2.50
___ 0-425-10516-4	YOUNG AT HEART #421 Jackie Leigh	$2.50

Available at your local bookstore or return this form to:

 SECOND CHANCE AT LOVE
THE BERKLEY PUBLISHING GROUP, Dept. B
390 Murray Hill Parkway, East Rutherford, NJ 07073

Please send me the titles checked above. I enclose _____. Include $1.00 for postage and handling if one book is ordered; add 25¢ per book for two or more not to exceed $1.75. CA, NJ, NY and PA residents please add sales tax. Prices subject to change without notice and may be higher in Canada. Do not send cash.

NAME _____

ADDRESS _____

CITY _____ STATE/ZIP _____

(Allow six weeks for delivery.)

Highly Acclaimed
Historical Romances From Berkley

_____ 0-425-10006-5   **Roses of Glory**
$3.95   by Mary Pershall
From the author of <u>A Triumph of Roses</u> comes a new novel about
a knight and his lady whose love defied England's destiny.

_____ 0-425-09472-3   **Let No Man Divide**
$4.50   by Elizabeth Kary
An alluring belle and a handsome, wealthy shipbuilder are drawn
together amidst the turbulence of the Civil War's western front.

_____ 0-425-09218-6   **The Chains of Fate**
$3.95   by Pamela Belle
Warrior and wife, torn apart by civil war in England, bravely battle
the chains of fate that separate them.

_____ 0-515-09082-4   **Belle Marie**
$3.95   by Laura Ashton
A tempestuous saga of a proud Southern family who defied the
rules of love—and embraced their heart's wildest desires.

Available at your local bookstore or return this form to:

THE BERKLEY PUBLISHING GROUP
Berkley • Jove • Charter • Ace
THE BERKLEY PUBLISHING GROUP, Dept. B
390 Murray Hill Parkway, East Rutherford, NJ 07073

Please send me the titles checked above. I enclose _____. Include $1.00 for postage
and handling if one book is ordered; add 25¢ per book for two or more not to exceed
$1.75. CA, NJ, NY and PA residents please add sales tax. Prices subject to change
without notice and may be higher in Canada. Do not send cash.

NAME _____

ADDRESS _____

CITY _____ STATE/ZIP _____

(Allow six weeks for delivery.)